Amy Cross is the author of more than 250 horror, paranormal, fantasy and thriller novels.

OTHER TITLES BY AMY CROSS INCLUDE

1689
American Coven
Angel
Anna's Sister
Annie's Room
Asylum
B&B
Bad News
The Curse of the Langfords
Daisy
The Devil, the Witch and the Whore
Devil's Briar
Eli's Town
Escape From Hotel Necro
The Farm
Grave Girl
The Haunting of Blackwych Grange
The Haunting of Nelson Street
The House Where She Died
I Married a Serial Killer
Little Miss Dead
Mary
One Star
Perfect Little Monsters & Other Stories
Stephen
The Soul Auction
Trill
Ward Z
Wax
You Should Have Seen Her

CRY OF THE WOLF

THE HORRORS OF SOBOLTON BOOK SEVEN

AMY CROSS

This edition
first published by Blackwych Books Ltd
United Kingdom, 2024

Copyright © 2024 Blackwych Books Ltd

All rights reserved. This book is a work of fiction.
Names, characters, places, incidents and businesses are
the product of the author's imagination or are
used fictitiously. Any resemblance to actual persons,
living or dead, or to actual events or locations,
is entirely coincidental.

Also available in e-book format.

www.amycross.com
www.blackwychbooks.com

CONTENTS

PROLOGUE
page 15

CHAPTER ONE
page 21

CHAPTER TWO
page 31

CHAPTER THREE
page 39

CHAPTER FOUR
page 49

CHAPTER FIVE
page 57

CHAPTER SIX
page 65

CHAPTER SEVEN
page 73

CHAPTER EIGHT
page 81

CHAPTER NINE
page 89

CHAPTER TEN
page 101

CHAPTER ELEVEN
page 109

CHAPTER TWELVE
page 117

CHAPTER THIRTEEN
page 125

CHAPTER FOURTEEN
page 133

CHAPTER FIFTEEN
page 141

CHAPTER SIXTEEN
page 149

CHAPTER SEVENTEEN
page 157

CHAPTER EIGHTEEN
page 165

CHAPTER NINETEEN
page 173

CHAPTER TWENTY
page 181

CHAPTER TWENTY-ONE
page 189

CHAPTER TWENTY-TWO
page 197

CHAPTER TWENTY-THREE
page 205

CHAPTER TWENTY-FOUR
page 213

CHAPTER TWENTY-FIVE
page 221

CHAPTER TWENTY-SIX
page 229

CHAPTER TWENTY-SEVEN
page 237

CHAPTER TWENTY-EIGHT
page 245

CHAPTER TWENTY-NINE
page 253

CHAPTER THIRTY
page 261

CRY OF THE WOLF

PROLOGUE

SHE RAN FAST, FASTER than she'd ever run before, faster than she ever realized she *could* run. All she knew was that she had to get away from him before -

Suddenly she slipped, or the muddy ground gave way, or she lost her balance – or perhaps all of those things happened at once. Whatever the cause, she tumbled and rolled, letting out a couple of pained gasps before scraping to a halt in the darkness.

Immediately trying to get up, she felt a sharp pain in the small of her back; she paused for a fraction of a second, waiting to see whether the pain would spread, and then she hauled herself onto her feet.

Reaching out, she felt the soft, damp bark of a nearby tree, and she realized in that moment that the air was already getting so much colder. She could hear her own frantic breaths, and her chest was positively heaving as she tried to get more air into her lungs.

After a few seconds she realized that she could hear something else, too: her own heartbeat, hammering in her chest with such force that she worried it might explode. Still, hearts didn't explode, she was fairly sure of that fact, although now she was starting to wonder. Ordinarily she would have asked her mother all about that, but asking her mother anything wasn't an option right now. For the first time in her life, she had to make her own decisions and work things out for herself. Turning, she began to look around what she assumed was a small clearing in the forest.

She could see nothing, and she could hear nothing – at least nothing from outside her own body.

The darkness stared back at her, threatening to unleash *him* at any moment. And then it would all have been in vain, every frantic second since her mother had shoved her out through the cabin's front door and had screamed in her ear with a frantic, ragged voice that sounded as if had torn the back of her throat.

"Run!" she heard the voice shouting, even now. "Eloise, get out of here before he -"

A shiver ran through her bones as she recalled the absolute terror in her mother's words. Part of her felt bad for running, but she knew that she'd had no choice.

"I'll be right behind you," her mother had said softly, just a few minutes before her escape. "I promise. But... if I'm not, Eloise, then you have to keep running anyway. Do you understand me? Run like your life depends on it."

"What if you don't come?"

"I will. I swear to you. Even if it takes a little longer than I'd like, eventually I'll come and find you."

At the time those words had been comforting, but now she realized that there had been such fear in her mother's voice, almost as if...

Almost as if her promise had been a lie.

Hearing a cracking sound, Eloise turned and looked to her left. The forest had fallen silent again, but she was already convinced that he must be nearby. Backing away, she bumped against another tree, then another, before turning and hurrying through the darkness. She slammed against yet another tree, almost winding herself, but she kept going and held her arms up in a desperate attempt to protect her face from sharp overhanging branches. In the chaos of the dark forest, she felt as if she was losing track of the world.

"Where are we going to run to?" she remembered asking earlier that night.

"The town."

"What town?"

"It's not far from here," her mother had explained. "Not too far, anyway. There are people there who can help us... if we can find them. I don't know, a lot might have changed. If it's changed too much, we'll find a car and we'll get the hell away from Sobolton."

"What's Sobolton?"

"It's the town," her mother had said, before pausing again and then leading her to the front door. "Okay, I think this is our chance. Eloise. We won't have another, not ever, so we need to get this right."

That moment seemed so long ago now. Stumbling yet again, Eloise almost fell, but this time she managed to stay on her feet. She felt a pain in her left knee, as if she'd almost torn something, but she pushed through that pain as she desperately tried to spot lights somewhere ahead. She wasn't even sure what a town looked like, or what one was; all she knew was the scraps of information she'd picked up from her mother.

"How will we find the town?" she'd asked earlier. "Do you know the way?"

"Sort of. But there'll be lights."

"What kind of lights?"

"More lights than you've ever seen in your life."

"More lights than the stars?"

"In a different way, yes." In that moment, she'd carefully opened the cabin's front door and pushed Eloise out into the cold night air. "Okay," she'd continued, "when I say run..."

As the ground suddenly dipped beneath her, Eloise let out a gasp and dropped down onto one knee. She managed to just about stay up, and she quickly set off again, rushing through the forest. After a few steps the ground began to rise again, which seemed like a good thing even though in truth she had no idea what was good and what was bad. In that moment, alone in the forest, all she wanted was to hear her mother's voice calling out to her, to know that she wasn't alone and to -

Suddenly the ground vanished entirely. Before she had a chance to stop herself, Eloise tumbled down through what felt – for a few seconds – like a void. And then, just as she wondered whether she'd run off the end of the world itself, she slammed against the hard ground below and her head hit an exposed root with enough force to knock her out cold.

For the next few minutes she lay unconscious in the darkness. Eventually a creaking sound could be heard, followed by another, and finally a wolf – thin and frail – stepped cautiously into view, sniffing the air as it approached Eloise's crumpled form.

CHAPTER ONE

IN THE BEGINNING, THERE was darkness. And then, seemingly out of nowhere, there came light.

The heat was immense, burning so fast and so strong that at first nothing could exist. For the earliest few milliseconds a thick patch of energy twisted around itself before starting to expand, spreading out into the ether. Had anyone been there to witness this vast explosion, they might have heard what sounded like screams ringing out at the heart of it all, although they might well have ignored those screams and assumed that they were merely a trick of the mind; or, instead, they might have tried to discern a voice, to pick out words in the maelstrom. But there was no-one to hear the sound, and there would be no-one to hear anything for many millions of years to come. The universe had burst into existence and was now screaming as it grew.

As the heat began to fade, the first atoms formed.

***

A ball of molten rock, cooling in the emptiness of space, hung in the orbit of a growing rumbling star. This ball of rock wasn't entirely spherical, not yet, but enough matter had gathered to at least give it some semblance of its future shape. In the silence of the void, the rock was at least able to hold together as its mottled surface began to form. The process would take many more millions and millions of years. For now, the planet – if it could even be called a planet at such an early stage of its existence – looked for all the world as if it had been scooped up by a giant hand and crudely patted into shape.

***

As the planet cooled and an atmosphere began to form, the first life emerged. Organic matter drifted through huge lakes on the surface, waiting for the first spark of life. Tectonic plates shifted beneath the surface, ripping apart the earliest attempts to form mountains and valleys.

Occasionally more rocks arrived from the void beyond, plummeting into the atmosphere and crashing down with immense power, cracking the land open and sending huge rivers of lava flowing down the sides. Massive plumes of dust were thrown into the air, sometimes blocking out the sun's early light for thousands of years. Over time the pools of organic matter began to settle, and eventually the first flicker of life started to spread. More time passed, and soon there were small creatures living in the pools; the creatures changed endlessly, sometimes combining and sometimes dividing, until finally one broke through the surface and began to crawl up onto the damp, warm rocks.

***

After millions of years spent roaring through the emptiness of space, a huge chunk of rock began to fall down into the planet's atmosphere. Burning at the edges, the rock plummeted toward a continent filled with the earliest large life-forms. Thick black smoke began to billow from the rock's edges and flames roared across its surface, lighting up the sky.

Down on the ground, many of the reptiles

looked up. They had no idea what they were seeing, but on some instinctive level they understood that it was bad. Panic set in and great herds began to move as one, trampling over one another in a desperate attempt to get as far as possible from the fireball. The ground thundered under the impact of millions of feet, but in truth there was nowhere for them to run and nowhere they could hide. They could already feel the approaching roar of extinction.

When the rock hit the ground, a set of vast cracks tore through the land. Many of the reptiles died instantly, but many more lingered as thick dust filled the air and the sun was once again choked off. This time there would be no quick respite, and over time the last of the creatures began to die off. Soon there was almost no life left at all, and the planet lay barren once more.

***

They came from the trees.

Eventually, many thousands of miles from the asteroid's impact site, a creature missed its footing and slid down, finally landing with a thud on the ground. Startled, the animal looked around, terrified that danger might arrive from any direction. Instead it saw only the silent forest floor, and after a moment the creature began to crawl forward. Ready to climb back up into the trees at any moment, it nevertheless felt brave enough to at least venture a few meters forward.

High above, the creature's family screamed out a warning, convinced that lethal threats were going to come at any moment. On the ground, however, the first creature pushed on, clambering past the nearest trees as it began to explore this strange new world. And the longer this creature spent exploring, the more emboldened the others became, until they too began to climb down the trees so that they could also take to the land.

***

They walked for years, for decades, for generations. Spreading across the world, they regularly came into contact with others who had gone before them. Sometimes these encounters were peaceful, but more often than not they ended in blood and violence.

Yet there were enough of them to keep going.

They were seeking food and places to rest. Few of them had yet realized that they could create settlements, so for the most part they consumed and moved on. Sometimes they saw flashes of light moving in the sky, and they told themselves that other beings must live up there; over time they developed the ability to discuss these sights, and eventually they concluded that the lights must be important. They soon came up with a word for these higher beings.

Gods.

After all, how else had the world come into existence in the first place? Whenever food was scarce, or whenever floods came, some of the creatures came up with the idea of making offerings to these gods. Sometimes the gods listened and sometimes they didn't, but temporary setbacks weren't enough to stem the advance of the creatures.

So they spread and they spread, sometimes traveling across vast seas, often pushed back by changes to the weather. The vast terrain – mountains and rivers and valleys – served to funnel them, directing them along the paths of least resistance, threading them through a world that had not yet been divided up by the whims of men with maps. Many of the creatures died, but enough persisted that gradually they moved further north and further east. They believed that there was no limit, that they could keep going forever and never run out of land.

They were almost right.

***

When the cold came, many froze to death.

Huddled together in makeshift camps, around fires that they had only just learned how to make properly, they offered more and more to the gods. In almost every case, the gods put their fingers in their ears so that they wouldn't hear the desperate cries of the creatures scrabbling around for warmth on the ground.

The cold lasted for many generations. Any other creatures would surely have given up, yet something strange began to happen. The harsher the conditions, the more determined some of these particular creatures became to keep pushing onward, to explore and to find new expanses of land. For a growing number of them, any attempt to hold them back was taken as a personal insult, and they sought to prove the doubting mountains wrong by climbing over them, and to simply ignore the barren plains' attempts to starve them away. And when the temperature eventually began to rise again, the creatures found that the ice was slowly receding.

They had won, at least for now.

Gradually the seas rose, restricting the space that the creatures could use. Some of them kept going to the east, and eventually they began to cross a narrow land bridge that would soon be washed away entirely. Finally one of the creatures stopped for a moment, as if he sensed that trouble lay ahead. He watched the untamed land before him, and after a few more seconds he began to tentatively step forward, becoming the first of his kind to ever set foot in this place.

Behind him, others saw his bravery and began to follow.

***

Stopping for a moment, the wolf leaned down and began to inspect a disturbance that had cut through the mud. Unaccustomed to such signs, the wolf sniffed the dirt and immediately pulled back. He wasn't sure what he'd found, exactly, but he knew that the scent was entirely unfamiliar. Something different, something unknown, had passed this way.

Different was bad.

Unknown was bad.

Hearing a distant cry, the wolf looked toward the clifftop. He hesitated for a few seconds, but he knew that he had to see what was happening.

Staying low, he began to crawl across the icy, rocky ground until he reached the edge, and when he looked down he saw several upright figures moving through the valley. The wolf's eyes narrowed slightly; he had no idea what these creatures were, yet in some way he understood that they were trouble.

For one thing, they seemed to be moving in a kind of pack, and for another they appeared to be organized. No wolf in this land had ever seen a human before, and this particular wolf felt a growing sense of fear starting to spread through his gut. Finally one of the humans looked up, and the wolf met its gaze briefly before turning and hurrying away. The wolf had no idea what the humans wanted, but he had already made up his mind to stay away from them as much as possible. And as the wolf reached the next outcrop, he turned and looked back. Sure enough, some of the humans had already begun to climb after him.

Every fiber of the wolf's being shuddered as he turned and hurried away. He knew that the humans would keep coming, and that in that case he and his kind would have to keep running. The two species simply couldn't ever mix.

CHAPTER TWO

Sobolton, USA – Today...

THE LIFE SUPPORT SYSTEM let out a series of regular, continuous beeps. The same beeps had been filling the room for several hours now, disturbed only by the sound of nurses' rustling uniforms as they occasionally checked on one or other of the drips.

"John," Robert Law said finally, standing in the doorway and watching as Lisa Sondnes remained unconscious in the hospital bed, "I *really* have to insist that you -"

"Later."

"But -"

"Later, Bob."

"Later's no good," Robert continued. "She's not going to wake up in the next few hours. She's got enough drugs in her system to knock out a racehorse. Meanwhile, we have to look at -"

"I have deputies for that," John replied, interrupting him yet again, keeping his eyes very much fixed on Lisa's face. "I need to be here when she wakes up."

"And I just told you, we can more or less schedule that," Robert said, struggling to contain his sense of frustration. "Lisa Sondnes is just one part of a very big puzzle, and at least now we know where she is. Meanwhile there's a terrified little girl in a nearby room, and Tommy's not out of the woods yet, and John... I need to take a look at your hands."

Glancing down, John saw his own twisted and broken fingers. The pain had become so natural now that he'd been able to screen it out, yet in his heart of hearts he knew that he needed to get himself checked over. He'd been through one hell of an ordeal out there in the forest, but sheer adrenaline was keeping him going and he worried that if he stopped – if he even slowed down for so much as a second – he might never be able to get started again.

"Time is of the essence," Robert continued.

"It can wait."

"The bones -"

"How's she alive, Bob?" he asked, cutting him off one more time, this time turning to look at him. "You conducted an autopsy on that little girl. How can she be up and walking around?"

"I don't know," Robert replied, lowering his voice a little as if he was worried that one of the nurses might overhear. "Believe me, that particular development has grabbed my attention too. I can tell that you've been through some stuff tonight, John, and I know it's not a competition but... there are a few things that I really should tell you when we get the chance to sit down and swap stories."

"I'm not leaving Lisa's side."

"She won't be awake for at least twenty-four hours."

"Says the man who conducted an autopsy on a girl who's now chatting away in an examination room."

"That's a low blow, John," Robert replied, "and not one that I'd expect from you." He took a moment to clear his throat, and then both men turned and looked back over at Lisa as she remained flat on her back in the bed. "I never thought this day would come, you know. Not really. I doubt anyone did. We all just thought Lisa Sondnes was lost out there somewhere, never to be found. Now to have her back, and alive... when word gets out across the town, there are gonna be a whole load of questions. Hell, this might even make the national news."

"Which is precisely why I need to come up with answers, and fast," John said firmly. "Go and talk to that Eloise girl. Listen to whatever she's got to say for herself and find out what the hell's going on with her."

"Yes, Boss," Robert muttered, rolling his eyes before turning and starting to limp away. "Remind me, when did I become your assistant, again? I think I must have missed that particular promotion."

Ignoring his friend's words, barely hearing them at all, John continued to watch Lisa. He knew full well that she was sedated, but he simply couldn't bring himself to leave the room, not after the entire town had spent twenty years wondering about her disappearance. He knew that when she finally woke up, he had to be the first person to speak to her, and that he had to find out how she'd ended up hidden away under a hatch in a remote cabin. Lisa Sondnes, he felt quite sure, was the key to everything.

Next to that, the pain in his broken fingers seemed like nothing at all.

***

"Where's Mommy?" Eloise asked softly, as she sat on the end of a table in one of the hospital's many examination rooms. "Can I see her now?"

"Not quite yet," Robert replied, trying to sound as calm and authoritative as possible. In truth, he'd never been too good at talking to children, but he figured he was going to have to do his best. "Sweetheart, I know this isn't the best time, but I have a lot of questions for you. Do you remember any of the things you were saying to me earlier tonight?"

She thought for a moment, scrunching her nose slightly, before shaking her head.

"You don't, huh?" Robert said. "Okay, that's fine. The last thing I want to do is push you, but... you said some pretty crazy stuff. You were trying to warn me. Does any of that ring a bell?"

She thought again, and then – once more – she shook her head.

"You don't remember any of that, do you?" he continued. "Interesting. You certainly seemed... different for a little while back there. Almost like it wasn't you talking through your mouth. Does that make any sense?"

"I don't know what you mean," she replied, and now she sounded as if she was close to tears. "My head hurts. When can I see Mommy?"

"Well, she's having a much-needed sleep right now," he explained, "because she's been... busy. So have you, from what I can tell. But what you have to understand is that your mom is receiving the best treatment possible, and right now we're having to prioritize her recuperation so that her long-term prognosis improves." He paused. "Am I using words that are too long for you?"

"I don't know," she said, lowering her voice a little. "Maybe."

"Yeah, I figured," he said with a sigh, before watching her for a moment longer. He'd been struggling for a while now to work out exactly what to make of her, but slowly the truth was dawning even if the revelation made very little sense. "You're just a kid."

Sniffing back tears, Eloise stared up at him.

"It's true," he continued, as if he could scarcely believe the words that were leaving his lips. "You're a... kid. You're a child."

"I'm sorry," she whimpered.

"No, don't be sorry," he replied. "Never be sorry. It's not a bad thing, it's just... surprising, after some of the things you said to me before."

"I want my mommy," she sobbed.

"And I'll get you to her," he insisted, suddenly overwhelmed by a profound sense of pity. "I swear, the moment she wakes up, I'll take you straight to her. I'm sure you'll be the first person on her mind just as soon as we bring her round."

"I miss her," she explained, sniffing back more tears. "I'm just scared that she'll be mad at me."

"Why would she be mad at you?" he asked.

"Because I ran away," she continued. "Because I got scared and... I ran away when I should have stayed with her. She told me to run, but I still should have stayed, it's just that I was so scared and he..."

Her voice trailed off.

"What were you scared *of?*" Robert asked. "Eloise, it's okay, you can tell me anything. You're never going to be in trouble, not here. We're all just so pleased that you're with us and that you're safe. Hell, frankly we're amazed. We don't really understand what's going on." He took a long, deep breath. "I'm terrible at explaining things," he added. "Sorry, that's just something that you and everyone else'll have to get used to. But the point is, I'm on your side, and so is everyone else here, so you don't have to hold anything back. I just really want to know how you ended up on my examination table, and how I was able to..."

He tried to work out how to finish that sentence, but he was worried that he might upset her.

"I don't know," she said cautiously. "I don't remember all of it. I was so scared when I ran away through the forest, and I didn't want to leave Mommy but I had to keep running because... because I was so scared that he'd catch up to me, because I knew he was so angry."

"Who?" Robert asked, determined to get to the truth even though he was worried about pushing her too hard. "Who was angry with you?"

"Daddy," she replied, and now the fear in her voice and in her eyes was impossible to miss. "I couldn't stop running. Daddy was really angry at me, and I was scared he might catch me."

CHAPTER THREE

The North American continent – early in the year 1050 AD...

VAST ROILING CLOUDS CHURNED in the sky above, filled with ever-darkening shades of gray and black but disturbed regularly by flashes of lightning. Occasionally these clouds seemed to briefly form faces, almost as if the gods themselves were looking down upon the pitiful sight before them.

At least, that was what Erik the Snub-nosed thought as he stood on the rocky ground with his sword drawn, waiting for others to catch up.

"Hurry!" he yelled in his native tongue, a tongue born thousands of miles away. "If you don't get here soon, we're leaving without you!"

That was a false threat. Erik would never leave anyone behind, but he had to make sure they understood the urgency of the situation.

Several hunched, terrified men and women were making their way across the clearing that led from the forest. Turning, Erik saw that the boat was ready. He felt a shimmer of dread at the thought of the long journey that awaited, but he knew that he and his fellow colonists had no choice. For around one generation now, they and others had toiled to make the land work in this strange new place, to bring peace and prosperity to a world that had initially seemed so full of possibility. Now they were being driven back by a combination of their own shortcomings and the hostile territory – not to mention local people and animals – that they had encountered. Nothing had worked.

The colony had failed. Erik and his men were returning to Europe, although first they had to make good their final escape.

"Get in the boat!" Erik snarled as the others finally reached him. He saw now that they'd been supporting a woman with a badly gnarled leg, and he flinched as he saw that her foot was entirely gone, leaving a bloodied trail. "What happened?"

"Another wolf!" Ragnar told him. "We were

wrong when we thought they'd abandoned the area! There are more of them than ever! It's almost as if they've been plotting an ambush!"

"You should have left me," the woman stammered, clearly delirious after losing so much blood.

"She's right," Erik said firmly, as thunder rumbled once again in the sky above. "You *should* have left her. She'll never survive the crossing back to our native lands."

"I'm not leaving her here," Ragnar replied. "Not on these heathen shores. And you'd never condone that, so don't even try to pretend that you would. We've all been in this together, right from the start!"

"The gods are angry with us," Erik pointed out, looking up at the clouds again. This time he saw no god-like faces in the swirling patterns, but as lightning rippled across the scene he felt sure that the gods' displeasure was filling the air all around. "They have every right to be. We have wasted not only our own work, but also the work and lives of those who came before us. We shall surely be welcomed back home as cowards and -"

Before he could finish, he spotted a dark shape appearing at the top of a rocky outcrop. He instinctively raised his sword as a large wolf stepped into view.

"Get her to the boat," he told Ragnar.

"But -"

"All of you!" he hissed. "That's an order. I'll fend this beast off and when you're ready, I'll come aboard. And then we set sail for home!"

The others began to make their way toward the waiting boat, splashing through the shallow water at the edge of the bay. The wolf, meanwhile, was following a trail of the woman's blood, and the beast showed little sense of fear as it made its way down from the rocks and began to approach the spot where Erik was standing.

"Are you after one last meal?" Erik called out angrily, already thinking of the dozen or so men, women and children who'd been lost to the increasingly ravenous wolves in the area. "Do you really think I'd let you sip even one more drop of our blood?"

Stopping for a moment, the wolf looked up at him. Saliva was dribbling from the creature's mouth as hunger rippled through its huge, muscular body. Erik knew by now how the wolves operated, and he could already see that this particular specimen was preparing to pounce; he adjusted his grip on the sword and tried to work out the best place to strike, supposing that he could simply attempt to slice open the monster's belly and leave its blood and guts to wash out across the rocks.

He'd seen many good, strong men fall in battle against these horrific beasts, but he told himself that he was going to avenge their deaths by cutting down one last horror of this strange new world.

"Erik!" a voice called out from the boat. "Hurry!"

"First I will empty this beast of all its blood," Erik snarled. "Only then shall -"

In that moment, catching him slightly by surprise, the wolf lunged low. Erik swung the sword down, missing the wolf and striking the rocks again, and in that moment the beast slammed against his legs and bowled him over. Dropping his sword, Erik fell down hard against the ground and immediately lashed out, hitting the side of the wolf's head and forcing it back before rolling onto his front and crawling across the rocks. Grabbing his sword, he turned around just as the wolf lurched forward again.

"Die!" Erik screamed, stabbing the sword's tip directly toward the animal and catching its shoulder. He felt the metal grind against bone, but the wolf slammed into his chest and damn near knocked all the air from his lungs.

"Erik!" another voice shouted from the boat.

"Stay there!" Erik gasped, barely able to get any words out at all as he attempted to turn his heavy sword and strike again. "Let me handle the -"

Suddenly the wolf bit his shoulder, driving its huge fangs straight through the thick leather of his tunic and cutting deep into his meat. As he felt hot blood erupting from the wound, and bones splintering beneath the surface, Erik leaned his head back and knew that his time as a great warrior had come to an end; after all, no man could ever recover from such a wound, but he also knew that he still had to finish the wolf off. Determined to strike before he lost too much blood, he tilted the sword around as lightning flashed across the furious clouds above, and finally he drove his weapon straight into the wolf's flank with such force that the blade burst out through the other side.

In that moment, Erik felt the wolf's grip on his shoulder starting to weaken, so he began to twist the blade as blood dribbled freely from the wound.

"Foul beast," he hissed, pulling harder and harder until his shoulder tore free from the wolf's gasping, panting jaws, "your death shall be my parting gift to this terrible place. I have half a mind to take your fur back with me as a symbol of man's mastery over your pathetic efforts."

He heard the wolf letting out a pained grunt. Erik had killed enough wild animals – not to mention men – to know when death had been secured. He began to slide the sword out from the wolf's flank, releasing a torrent of fresh blood that pumped from the wound, and now he felt a familiar sense of respect for his vanquished foe. As a great warrior, he had always known when to soften the anger of conflict and show proper respect to an enemy.

"I have beaten you," he purred softly, waiting for the right moment to throw the heavy beast aside, "but I shall bear the scar of this encounter for the rest of my life with pride. You were a worthy foe, and when sagas are written about my endeavors, I shall make sure that you are included."

With that, he began to push the wolf off, while preparing to rise from the rocky ground.

"You have not been my greatest rival," he continued, "but you certainly -"

In that moment the wolf lunged again, biting hard into the side of Erik's throat and then starting to rip away the flesh. Shocked, Erik reached out and grabbed the beast's jaws, desperately trying to break free, but he felt a rush of shame as he realized that – in one moment of complacency – he'd allowed this dying monstrosity to strike back. As more and more blood gushed from the side of his neck, he understood that now he would be dying along with his victim, that a great victory had been snatched away and now he was going to fall in this new world. He rolled over, still locked together with the creature, before starting to force himself up as the wolf continued to bite down on the side of his neck. Slowly he turned and looked toward the boat, and in his shaking right hand he raised his sword.

"To Valhalla!" he screamed. "To the glory of -"

A flash of lightning arced down from the sky, striking the sword and showering the area with sparks. Erik let out an agonized cry as he and the wolf were enveloped in a blast of light, and then they slumped down together as one huge smoldering pile of molten flesh and bone and metal.

As rain began to fall, the crew on the boat watched the shoreline, waiting for Erik to move. They glanced at one another, wondering exactly what had happened, before finally Ragnar jumped over the side and began to wade back toward the shoreline.

"Wait!" a man called out. "It's not safe!"

Ignoring those words, Ragnar hurried across the rocks. He looked around, but he saw no sign of any other wolves. When he reached the large shape on the ground, with rain falling harder and harder, he was horrified to see that the bolt of lightning seemed almost to have fused Erik to the wolf, turning them into a vast and bloodied lump of grotesquely combined muscle and meat, a kind of mocking amalgam of what had once been a man and had once been a wolf. The sword, meanwhile, had been charred and blackened almost beyond recognition, and had fallen onto the rocks nearby.

Slowly the man-wolf mass began to shift slightly, and Ragnar was horrified to see an eye blinking in the rain as it stared up at him.

"Ragnar!" one of the men from the boat shouted. "What do you see?"

A faint gasp emerged from the horrific mass on the ground, but Ragnar knew in that moment that he was seeing something ungodly, something that should not exist... and something that, if left alone in the rainy storm, would surely die within minutes.

"Ragnar!" the voice cried out again. "Tell us what you see!"

"Nothing!" he shouted, taking a step back before lowering his voice as he looked once more at the eye and wondered whether Erik might in some way be able to hear him. "I'm sorry," he whispered, "I... I'm so sorry."

With that, he turned and raced back across the rocks, quickly returning to the boat. He took one last moment to spit upon the water before ordering the crew to take their positions. Within minutes the boat had begun to set sail from the bay, beginning its long and uncertain attempt to recross the Atlantic and return to its home. On the shore of the new world, meanwhile, the vast clumped mass of man and wolf lay panting in the rain, trying desperately to retain its strength, laboring with each rasping breath that it tried to drag into its screaming lungs. The flow of blood had stopped, at least, and one eye continued to look out at the sea, cursing those who had departed and vowing vengeance should they or their descendants ever dare to return.

CHAPTER FOUR

Sobolton, USA – Today...

"SHE'S NOT COMING ROUND in the near future," Doctor Mackenzie said, standing on the other side of the bed and looking down at Lisa's face. "Even when she does -"

"Why not?" John asked, watching Lisa intently.

"There's a process that we have to go through," Mackenzie continued, her voice tense with the need to remain professional. "It doesn't matter how many times you ask me this, Sheriff Tench, the answer's not going to change. I'm sure Doctor Law told you much the same thing. I won't hurry things up or abandon my ethics just because it'd suit you and your investigation."

"Do you really think that's what I'm asking you to do?"

"Perhaps I've misunderstood," she suggested.

"Don't patronize me!" he barked, before taking a moment to check himself. "I'm sorry, I shouldn't have raised my voice. It's just that I've waited so long to find this woman, and now she's right here in front of me but..."

His voice trailed off.

"Would you like me to take a look at your hands?" the doctor asked after a few seconds. "They look like they're in a bad way."

"Later."

"There's nothing for either of us to do here right now."

"I told you, I'll get them checked later. I've already had Bob Law nagging me, I don't need to hear the same thing but in a Scottish accent."

"Okay, then," Mackenzie muttered, rolling her eyes as she turned and headed to the door. Stopping, she looked back at him. "You know, they say a watched pot never boils."

He glanced at her.

"The longer you leave your hands, the worse the damage is likely to be," she continued. "You'll be delaying your recovery by a significant amount of time, and I'd have thought that's something you'd like to avoid. It doesn't have to be me, it doesn't even have to be at this hospital, but you *need* to get them looked at. Meanwhile Lisa Sondnes will continue her recovery at her own pace, and I assure you that when there's even half a sign that she might wake up, you'll be the first to know."

With that, she stepped out of the room, leaving John to turn and look at Lisa's face again. He was still struggling to imagine how the happy, vibrant woman from old photographs could now be the frail, emaciated figure in the hospital bed; he could only assume that she must have been through something truly horrific in the twenty years since she'd vanished, although he couldn't quite believe that anyone could have spent all that time trapped in a small pit beneath the floor of a remote cabin.

Flexing his fingers, he felt a sharp pain in several of the joints, although he told himself that the damage didn't seem to be *that* bad. Certainly not as bad as he'd first thought, and he found that he could actually move some of the fingers in a way that hadn't been possible right after the accident. He flexed them again, and he told himself that the doctors were just fussing over nothing, that he'd get them checked out as soon as possible but that right now... right now he couldn't afford to waste a single moment.

***

"Now," Miriam Hodges said as she made her way across the parking lot, heading toward the diner's main entrance, "you know me, I don't like to gossip, but I've heard some strange stories about that man."

"Tell me about it," her friend Linda replied, checking her watch. "Everyone's going on about it, people are even sharing some of their theories in some of the group chats I'm part of. If you ask me, there are some rotten apples in this town and it's time we had a good clear-out."

"Fine chance, while we've got cops who can't even solve the most basic crimes," Miriam said, reaching out to open the door. "It's not as if -"

Stopping suddenly, she found that the diner's door was locked. This made no sense at all. She tried it a couple more times, but the bolt was firmly in place on the inside. The lights were on, and when she glanced at her watch she saw that the place should certainly have just opened for its early morning customers, yet for the first time in as long as she could remember Miriam realized that she might be denied her first coffee of the day.

"What's going on?" Linda asked, furrowing her brow. "Wendy's not ill, is she?"

"She wasn't ill yesterday."

"Did she say she was going to be ill today?"

"No."

"Then why's the place shut?"

Miriam tried the door yet again, as if she

still couldn't quite believe that it refused to budge. She peered at the gap between the door and the frame, and she was just about able to make out a thick black shape marking the spot where the bolt had been slid into the gap. For as long as she'd been working at the bank down the street, Miriam had been dropping by the diner to pick up coffee not only for herself but also for her co-workers. The idea that the diner had suddenly shut seemed utterly incomprehensible, and finally she tried the door again even though she knew there was no way for it to open.

"I don't like this," Linda said cautiously.

"Neither do I," Miriam replied, taking a step back and looking at the large windows running along the front and around the side of the building.

"You don't think something's... happened, do you?"

"I don't know what I think," Miriam said, before stepping off the path and starting to make her way along the grass while looking into the building.

"Do you see anything?" Linda called after her.

"Not yet. Go and look round the other side, will you?"

Hearing Linda's footsteps trudging away, Miriam reached the corner of the diner and stopped. She could see all the empty tables inside, but after a moment she spotted what appeared to be some dirty mugs on the counter. Although she was no expert, she felt sure that Wendy would never have left used mugs out overnight, and she couldn't help but worry that something really serious must have happened. She paused for a moment, trying to make sense of the madness, and somehow her brain just couldn't get past the fact that she *always* had her first coffee of the morning from the diner. That was simply her routine.

Anything else just seemed... barbaric.

And then she spotted the blood. She leaned a little closer to the glass, but already her heart was pounding as she saw that a small amount of blood had been left smeared against the side of the counter, almost as if a bloodied hand had tried to grab hold of something while the rest of its body was being dragged around the corner. She tried to convince herself that she was actually seeing some kind of sauce, that of course it wasn't blood, yet if anything the bloodiness of the stain was becoming more apparent with each passing second, almost as if -

Suddenly, round the other side of the building, Linda screamed.

Miriam had never heard anyone scream before – not in real life, at least – so for a moment she simply froze. As the scream petered out to become more of an anguished sobbing sound, however, she hurried around to the other side of the diner and found her friend stepping back from the window with a horrified expression on her face.

"What's wrong?" Miriam asked, rushing over and grabbing the sides of her arms, as much to try to hold her up as anything else. "Linda, what happened?"

Turning, she looked at the diner, and in that instant she saw something small, dark and bloodied smeared against the window. Letting go of Linda, she cautiously made her way over; some part of her mind recognized the item on the glass, yet she couldn't quite believe the horror until she finally stopped just inches from the window and found herself staring at a human eyeball, which had been partially ruptured as if smashed from behind. The pupil was broken, and the eyeball had been smeared against the other side of the glass with such force that it appeared to have stuck, while the remains of the optic nerve were hanging down like trailing strands.

The sight was so awful, and so bizarre, that at first Miriam was unable to process what she was seeing at all. And then, finally, she also screamed.

***

From inside the diner, the scream sounded distinctly more muffled. The coolers hummed gently, as they always hummed, but a persistent dripping sound could be heard coming from behind the counter.

Wendy's body was on the floor, torn to pieces and partially smeared across the tiles. Her liver had been ripped out and thrown against the wall, causing blood to dribble down; part of her ribcage had been torn away, while her head had been cracked open to reveal what remained of her brain.

CHAPTER FIVE

Canterbury, England – December 29th, 1170

"WHO ARE THEY?" EDWARD asked, watching as the four men made their way past his foundry, heading toward the cathedral. "What do they want?"

"I do not know," the monk Gervase replied cautiously, "but it can be nothing good. I only hope that they do not come directly on the king's word, for I fear that nobody in this place is minded to compromise." He sighed. "How much longer must this enmity between Archbishop Becket and King Henry continue?"

"What should we do?" Edward replied.

For a moment, lost for words, Gervase didn't know how to respond. He knew that these four knights were up to no good, that their mere presence at the cathedral was surely a sign that recent quarrels between the archbishop and the king were reaching a new level of acrimony. At the same time, he felt certain that no violence or quarrel could threaten the sanctity of the cathedral, and that a house of prayer would surely provide protection against the worst excesses of the king's men. No matter how bad things might get, nobody would ever dare to strike at such a hallowed and important place.

Yet a nagging sense of doubt was tugging at his chest. He knew full well that even the slightest misjudgment in such a situation could lead to the most terrible of events. Good decisions took time to take effect, but bad decisions could cause chaos in the blink of an eye.

"We should secure ourselves," one of the other monks said, emerging from a storehouse. "If they mean to take our blood -"

"We shall do no such thing without the archbishop's direct order," Gervase said firmly.

"But we're not safe!"

"We are in the safest place in all of England," Gervase replied, slightly frustrated by the other man's fears. "Do you truly believe that the Lord would allow this hallowed temple to be darkened by sin? Those four men would be traitors not only to the land but to God if they drew their swords here, and they know that full well. Do you actually think that we are in danger?"

"I for one am not staying to find out," Edward muttered, turning and hurrying toward the gate. "I wish you well, but I would advise that you should take greater care of your lives. I saw the gleam in the eyes of those men. They mean harm."

"What if he's right?" the other monk asked.

"Stand your ground," Gervase said, turning to him. "How many times do I have to tell you? The king and his men might have made some terrible mistakes of late, but even they would not stoop so low as to visit violence upon this most sacred of spaces." He turned and looked toward the grand, imposing cathedral that stood a short distance away, yet still that nagging doubt made itself known in his chest. "I refuse to believe that anyone, anywhere in the whole world, would be so wicked."

***

"Where is he?" the knight shouted, battering the door open and stepping through. In the cathedral's low light, he could already see Archbishop Thomas Becket kneeling in prayer at the altar. "There he is," he sneered, already drawing his sword. "The traitor does not know the danger he now faces."

"You think not?" Becket whispered, listening to the sound of the knights stepping closer but not yet rising or turning to them. "Then you are fools as well as villains."

"Get on your feet!" the first knight snapped angrily.

Becket hesitated for a moment, before slowly rising. He took a moment to adjust his robes, and then he turned to see the four knights who had arrived a little earlier, as well as a number of clerics who had now followed them into the cathedral. For a few seconds Becket felt a ripple of anger, but he quickly reminded himself that now of all times he had to remain strong, that he had to demonstrate the faith he had so often taught to other men.

"The king does not come himself?" he asked.

"Why would King Henry deign to come anywhere near this traitorous nest?"

"Such cruel words to describe the most magnificent palace of the Lord," Becket replied, before gesturing toward the walls. "Sir, why do you not set down your sword and instead marvel at the beauty of -"

"You're coming with us," the knight said angrily, interrupting him.

"I have no intention of going anywhere," Becket told him. "We are in the middle of our vespers. There is much to do here in the daily life of the church, and besides, King Henry has shown no great interest in listening to good counsel. Why, the king could be covered in ears from head to toe, and still I do not think he would listen."

"Traitorous filth!" the knight snarled.

"We could have barred your way," Becket pointed out. "We could have put up barricades and turned this house of prayer into a fortress, but we did not."

"You could never have stopped us!"

"Perhaps you are right, but we did not even make the attempt." Becket paused for a moment as he saw the other knights edging closer. "This is a house of the Lord."

"Do you think that gives you the right to treat King Henry with such contempt?" the knight asked. "Who are you, anyway, besides a low-born cleric risen to a position beyond your capabilities? The king has asked each of us how he has come to be treated so poorly. Now we arrive to show him that we are his loyal servants. And you, Becket, are going to come with us and see the king himself, so that you can explain your actions and beg for his mercy."

"In no manner am I going to do any such thing," Becket said through gritted teeth. "If the king wishes to speak to me, he knows where to find me. He can come here to this very spot. Assuming, of course, that he dares set foot in a place where wickedness and sin are soon found out."

He paused, but he was unable to resist a slight dig at his former friend.

"Does he fear," he added with a faint smile, "that his feet might burn on consecrated ground?"

"I tire of these words," the knight muttered, before nodding at his companions. "Drag the fool out. We shall take him by force."

The other knights stepped forward and grabbed Becket, trying to lead him out of the cathedral. Taking hold of a nearby pillar, Becket held firm and bowed his head, whispering a prayer as he felt the shadow of death moving ever closer.

"Finish this!" one of the knights hissed.

"Indeed I shall," the first knight replied, raising his sword and bringing the blade crashing down, slicing away part of Becket's scalp and sending blood splattering against the wall.

"He does not fall!" another voice cried out.

"He will," the first knight said, before striking Becket again, this time on the side of his head.

Still clinging to the pillar, Becket was just about able to remain on his feet even as blood flowed freely now down both sides of his head. He was still whispering, still praying even as his knees began to buckle.

"Still he does not fall!" one of the clerics gasped. "What have we done?"

"The third time shall be the charm," the first knight shouted, before swinging his sword yet again, this time dividing Becket's head almost in two, sending the top part crashing down.

Letting out a pained gasp, Becket fell back against the stones. Blood and brain matter flowed out from his desecrated skull, with pieces of broken bone washing away in the flow of whitish-red liquid that soon began to mix and gave the ground a purplish hue. A moment later, one of the clerics stepped forward and stamped hard on Becket's neck, and this action forced the remaining blood from the dying man's skull while also bringing a spluttering gasp from his lips.

"It is done!" the first knight sneered, looking down at the horrific sight.

"We can leave this place now," one of the other men added, as Becket's shuddering body finally fell still. "See for yourself. He shall not rise again. We can return to King Henry and tell him proudly that we have done our duty."

As the knights stormed away, several monks loitered nearby, horrified by what they had seen. Finally, once they were sure that the men with swords had departed, they began to nervously move forward, watching Becket's corpse in the hope that they might spot even the slightest hint of continued life. Gathering around him, however, they all saw very keenly now that he was surely dead.

"King Henry will pay for this," one of the monks said, his voice filled with shock. "I do not know how, or when, but I know it in my heart... he will pay for ordering the death of this holy martyr."

"He shall indeed," another monk replied, reaching down and picking up one of the many bloodied shards of skull that now lay on the ground, He turned the shard around, marveling at the horrific violence that had disturbed one of the holiest places in all of England. "And martyred he has truly been. Quickly, gather what you can of his remains. These are sure to become powerful relics."

CHAPTER SIX

Sobolton, USA – Today...

"HELLO, ELOISE. MY NAME is John Tench, and I really want to ask you a few questions. Do you think that would be okay?"

He waited, but the girl merely stared up at him with the same frightened expression she'd worn ever since he'd entered the room. Actually, that wasn't quite true; she'd been scared when he entered, but she'd only begun to look truly terrified once Doctor Law had excused himself for a few minutes.

Now, as he pulled a chair over and sat in front of the bed, John was once again reminded of his complete inability to actually talk to children. Sure, Robert Law claimed to have difficulties in this regard, but John knew that his own utter failure trumped all. Even when his own son Nick had been young, John hadn't known how to act around him, and the consequences there hadn't exactly been positive.

"I'm the sheriff here in Sobolton," he continued, trying to put her at ease. "Do you know what that means? It means that it's my job to investigate whenever anything doesn't quite seem right. You're not in any trouble, Eloise, but I think you might know a few things that would help me do my job a lot better. Do you understand now why I have to talk to you, even though..."

Glancing at his watch, he saw that the time was almost six in the morning. Light was starting to shine through the nearby windows, but any tiredness he felt was being smothered by an urgent need to get answers. He knew he was going to have to rest at some point, but he also knew that he had to strike while the case was still so fresh.

"A lot of people have been very worried about you," he told the girl. "A lot of people have been very confused, too. When we found you..."

For a moment, he thought back to the sight of her body beneath the ice. Logic and reason told him that this couldn't possibly be the same girl, that she couldn't have survived both that and an autopsy, yet he couldn't deny that she was sitting before him now and that she was clearly very much alive.

"Just to clear one thing up first," he continued, "can you tell me... I don't suppose you have a twin sister, do you? Someone who looks a lot like you?"

Eloise thought for a moment, before solemnly shaking her head.

"I didn't think so," John added, and then he took a deep breath. "That would be far too easy."

"Can I see Mommy now?" the girl whimpered.

"Soon," he told her.

"When?"

"Soon." He paused. "Believe me, we're all very keen for your mother to wake up."

"She told me she'd be right behind me," she replied. "Now I don't know whether she meant it. I think maybe..." Her voice trailed off for a few seconds. "I think maybe she was trying to save me."

"That's what I want to ask you about," he said cautiously. "Eloise, when we found you a few months ago, you were... I mean, this is going to sound quite strange but bear with me because... when we found you, you were in the ice. Do you know Drifter's Lake?"

"I'm not sure," she admitted. "Was I actually... *in* the ice?"

"You were frozen solid," he explained. "Eloise, the lake had frozen during the night, there was a very sudden cold snap and we actually had quite a bit of trouble getting you out. Now, ordinarily there wouldn't be much more we could do for you after that, except try to establish the circumstances that led to your... predicament."

"What does that word mean?"

"Well..." He took a moment to clear his throat. Having never been good with children, he wasn't sure now how much he could tell the girl. She seemed simultaneously both very smart and also childlike, almost naive. "It means that someone who's been trapped in ice for a number of hours would normally not have a very good prognosis. Sorry, that's another long word, it means... outlook."

"Was I dead?"

He opened his mouth to reply, but the directness of her question had caught him a little off-guard.

"I remember running," she continued, "and trying to get away through the forest. Mommy told me to try to get to the town." She looked around the room, watching the lights and the electronic displays with an almost awe-inspired expression of puzzlement. "I guess... this is the town, is it?"

"This is Sobolton."

"That's a funny name. What does it mean?"

"Well," he replied, "to be totally honest with you, I'm not sure. Next time I have a free moment, I'll have to look it up. It must come from somewhere."

"Mommy told me to come here," she added, before looking at him again. "She told me we'd try to be safe here, and that if we couldn't be safe here then we'd go somewhere else."

"I know this is a tough question," he replied, "but... exactly who were you running from?"

"We were running from Daddy," she told him, and now a hint of fear entered her voice. "Daddy was angry. Daddy was always angry, but last night... or the last night I remember before now... he was angrier than I'd ever seen him. And when Daddy gets angry, sometimes he does really bad things." She paused again. "I think that's how I was made."

***

Jessie's fingers hovered just above the keyboard, ready to type just as soon as her frazzled and sleep-deprived brain could work out exactly how to explain the night's events. So far, that task seemed completely impossible.

"Problem?"

Looking up, she saw Garrett emerging from one of the other rooms.

"Yeah, me too," he continued with a heavy sigh. "Come on, it's way past knocking off time for both of us. I don't know about you, but I feel like I could sleep for years. Like that Rip Van Winkle guy."

"Fairy-tales are the last thing we need right now," she replied, before looking back at the monitor. "How the hell am I supposed to sum up last night's events in one of these standardized reports? If I put down even one millionth of what really happened, I'll be dragged off to a psych ward faster than I can draw breath."

"Doctor Law said he'd back us up."

"Doctor Law's a barely-functioning alcoholic with serious issues of his own," she pointed out, clearly not impressed by that suggestion. "If we're relying on Doctor Law to bail us out, we're truly screwed."

"I just can't believe that we've got *the* Lisa Sondnes on our ward," he replied, wandering over to a nearby door and looking through at Lisa's unconscious body in the bed. "I mean, I've heard people talk about her over the years, and mentioning the fact that she's missing. I watch enough true crime documentaries to know that when people vanish for twenty years, the odds of them turning up alive are... slim."

The chair creaked as Jessie got to her feet. Walking over to join him, she too looked at Lisa for a moment before heading to the bed and checking the monitors.

"And in the extreme cases where they *do* turn up," Garrett continued, making his way to the other side of the bed and checking the drip, "they're not the same."

"I guess being held prisoner by some maniac must screw a person's head up pretty permanently," she suggested, bending down to adjust one of the machines. "I mean, that's what's happened here, right? Some lunatic had her... chained up in a dungeon or something like that."

"I overheard Sheriff Tench talking to Doctor Law," Garrett said, turning to her. "She was being kept in some cabin in the forest. That forest's creepy enough at the best of times. And did you see that little girl they had with them? She's Lisa's daughter, which only adds a whole new level of insanity to the whole situation."

"Maybe that explains Lisa still being alive, though," Jessie replied, as they both headed to the door. "Parents can do crazy things when their kids are in danger. It's almost like a superpower. Anyway, I'm glad that's not our problem. You're right, I'm just gonna type up the basics and file the report, and then I'm out of here. I've got two days off, and I don't know about you but I intend to try to forget about last night as much as possible."

"Ditto," he said as they reached the desk.

"Damn it," she muttered, checking her pockets. "Where did my scissors go? I swear I had them earlier. Great, that's another thing I need to worry about. That can be something for next time

I'm here, though. After last night, I just want to vegetate for a few days. Screw everything else in the whole goddamn world."

As they continued to talk at the desk, back in the room Lisa was still on the bed with various wires and leads connecting her to the machines. Her left hand, however, had slipped slightly beneath the covers; a moment later the hand moved out slightly, revealing a small pair of scissors held firmly in her grip. Meanwhile her eyelids opened by just a few millimeters, allowing her to look at the door as she waited for her chance to escape.

CHAPTER SEVEN

Plymouth, England – 1686...

HENRY PUSHED THROUGH THE haunting crowd, struggling to find his way along the overflowing dock. Night had fallen several hours earlier, but torches burned on posts as the late-night market men peddled their wares. All around Henry, other men hollered and cried out, getting in his way but basically seeking the same thing that he himself was after.

Freedom.
Escape.
A new life.

"I'm looking for Alexander Humford," he said as he squeezed through a small gap and found himself next to several men who – like him –

looked rough and exhausted. He briefly spotted his own reflection in a nearby mirror before turning to the others again. "Does anyone here know of an Alexander Humford?"

"And who's Alexander Humford when he's at home?" one of the men asked, eyeing him with suspicion.

"Please, I'm only asking," Henry continued. "I know very little about him, save that he's said to be a portly, stout fellow who runs a desk somewhere here near the water. If any of you know where I might find him, I would be -"

"Move!" an angry voice yelled, and all the men turned to see several figures forcing their way on horseback through the crowd. "In the name of His Majesty King James, you will move or you will be killed!"

"Stand aside," another men called out, pressing the others back further until they were almost crushed against one another. "The king's men are coming through!"

"The king's men are *always* coming through," a bearded man murmured as he watched from nearby. "The sooner we're rid of the king and all his men, the better."

"Hush," another man whispered. "Better not let anyone else hear you say that, else you'll be clad in irons and thrown headfirst into the water."

"This can't last much longer," the bearded

man said darkly. "England won't stand for it. Argyll won't be the last. There'll be more attempts to depose him, and more and more, until eventually someone'll succeed. It's not that long ago that we overthrew the lot of them, you'll recall. I'm not sure why we ever reversed that decision."

"Please," Henry said, as the king's men continued to ride past, "I'm merely looking for Alexander Humford, and it's a matter of the utmost urgency. If one of you would be so kind as to let me know where I can find him, I shall be on my way."

"*I* know where you can find him," an older man said, his voice trembling with pain.

Henry turned to him.

"Keep going that way," the man continued, pointing along the dock toward some larger buildings at the far end. "Ask when you get to the eaves, and someone'll surely direct you right to him. Mind that you're sure of your decision, though, for there are rumors about Mr. Humford and his dealings. Some say that he's not to be trusted."

"Thank you," Henry said, turning and immediately forcing his way through the crowd again. The rest of his words were soon lost in the din.

"There's only one reason why anyone ever comes looking for Alexander Humford," the old man mused, ignored by the others as they crowded together with their backs turned to him, "and that's because they want to take their leave of this fetid isle for good. And I for one can't say that I blame them."

***

"Mr. Humford? I'm sorry to disturb you, but... are you Alexander Humford?"

"That very much depends," the large man said, not looking up from the papers he was studying at a desk in the far corner of a dank little office. "Who wants to know, and more importantly, how much money have you got?"

"I've been told that you can... arrange safe passage to the Americas."

"You have, have you?"

"I've been told that you can get people onto ships bound to cross the Atlantic," Henry continued. "It's -"

"There's no difficulty in that," the man grumbled, still not looking up. "Any fool can get himself employed on one of the vessels that leave here. You don't need a man such as myself to arrange that."

"But I have a family."

At this, the large man finally looked up.

"I have a wife," Henry continued, "and two daughters, and I must take them with me."

"Leave them behind. Start fresh."

"I can't do that. I would never leave them."

"Are you a fool?"

"Why would you ask me that?"

"Do you know how dangerous this journey would be for all of you?" Humford asked. "Even the crossing itself is filled with peril. Disease, storms, starvation... all these things can kill you, and that's even before you've had to deal with your fellow passengers." He began to smile. "Then there are the rats."

"I know these things," Henry replied, "yet I have no choice. We must go."

"Why *must* you go?"

"We... are not safe here."

"Have you done something?" Humford replied. "Are you wanted by the authorities? For if you are, I shall not arrange safe passage for a criminal."

"It's nothing of that nature," Henry told him, before pausing for a moment. "In truth, it's a matter of worship. We have our ways, but those ways are becoming increasingly unpopular and I fear that the wind will not change direction anytime soon. I am a good husband and a good father, and I have to protect my family. The way I see it, the best way to do that is to take them to the Americas so that we can start a new life there."

"Do you think it will be easy?"

"Not at all," Henry said firmly. "I've heard

the same tales as everyone else."

"You'll do well to leave the immediate area when you land," Humford told him. "Go inland when you reach the new world. That might seem to be against all logic, but if you have a family, you'll be wanting to get away from other people."

"I understand that."

"You won't receive much in the way of a welcome anywhere," Humford continued. "There are savages out there. They're ungodly creatures that populated the Americas long before we arrived to show them what's what. The job of extinguishing them is taking much longer than anyone could have expected. You could fight them, but you'd do best to just stay away from them altogether."

"I have no quarrel with anyone," Henry explained, "so long as he in turn leaves me alone."

"A wise approach," Humford murmured.

"I have this," Henry said, tipping the contents of a small pouch onto the desk, revealing a meager collection of gold. "Will it be enough?"

"Where did you get this from?"

"That is my concern."

"Is it stolen?"

"It is not. As God is my witness, Sir, I am no thief. I am honest and I have spent time gathering my resources so that I can make this trip." He waited for a response, but already he worried that his pleas might be falling upon deaf ears. "Sir, please," he continued finally, "if you have no mercy for me, then at least have pity on my wife and daughters. They are not safe here, and they never will be. I would rather take them to the uncertainty of the new world, than let them stay here in the certain horrors of the old."

Humford stared at the gold for a moment longer, before gathering it together and then sliding it into a small box that he took from one of the drawers.

"Does that mean you'll help us?" the man asked.

"It means that if you and your family can be here at this time tomorrow," Humford replied, "then there will be space for you on a vessel that sails that night for Holland. Once there, you will be introduced to a man who can arrange the rest of your journey. This will not be quick, and it might take six months before you reach your destination."

"Six months?" Henry asked forlornly.

"Or longer."

"Longer?"

Now he sounded positively desperate.

"Take it or leave it," Humford said, picking up a quill and then drawing a piece of paper closer. "Now, I'm a busy man and I have no desire to debate this matter endlessly. If you won't take those four spots on the vessel that sails tomorrow, others surely will. Am I to put your names down or not?"

Henry thought for a moment, wondering whether there might be some better option, yet in truth he knew that any further delay might well mean death. The situation in England was deteriorating rapidly, and he feared that soon a new war might break out that would make the previous battle against the king's father seem like nothing more than a mere skirmish. Six months was a long time to spend on any journey, but he told himself that once he reached the Americas, he would find a way to start a new life there – preferably far away from other men.

"My name is Henry," he said finally, and he watched as Humford began to take notes. "My wife is Clara, and our daughters are Belle and Mary."

"Henry," Humford murmured as he wrote, "Clara, Belle and... Mary. And what is your second name?"

"Sobolton," he replied, as his eyes burned with fear and anticipation of whatever the new world might hold for him and his family. "My name is Henry Sobolton."

CHAPTER EIGHT

Sobolton, USA – Today...

"OKAY, WHAT HAVE WE got here?" Toby asked, still adjusting his belt as he made his way toward the diner. Already a small crowd had gathered nearby, held back by yellow tape.

"I thought you were taking the day off," Sheila replied, turning to him.

"Yeah, well, it's all hands on deck," he told her as he followed her up the steps and into the diner. "I'm fine, I was a little queasy last night but I think I know what caused that. I'm all better now and -"

Stopping suddenly, he saw the eyeball smushed against a nearby window. Instinctively reaching down and touching the front of his belly, he quickly began to lose all the color in his face.

"Are you *sure* you're okay?" Sheila asked.

"I'll be fine," he said firmly, before taking a deep breath and heading over to look at the eyeball. "Is this from the waitress? What's her name again?"

"Wendy," Sheila told him, as she checked her clipboard. "I've got all her details here."

"What the hell is going on with this town lately?" Toby asked, peering more closely at the eyeball as the optic nerve continued to dangle down. "What's this obsession with... removing eyes?"

"Beats me," Sheila said, "but the rest of her isn't much better. Is Sheriff Tench on his way?"

"I sent a message to him," Toby replied, turning to her, "but I couldn't actually talk to him. I'm pretty sure he's tied up right now, but when he finds out about this... I'm not sure, but do you think it could be related to what happened to Tommy?"

"I don't know what I think right now," she told him, "but... you really need to see Wendy. Or what's left of her. Someone really went to town on the poor woman."

"Alright," Toby muttered, heading back over. "Let me see the -"

Before he could finish, he heard a squelching sound, and he turned just in time to see that the eyeball had begun to come unstuck from the window. He and Sheila watched as the eyeball began to slowly slide down the glass, leaving a smeared trail in its wake.

"Should we try to stop it?" Toby asked.

"Why?"

"Because it's... evidence?" he suggested, clearly at something of a loss. "Did you take photos?"

"Not yet."

The eyeball continued to slide down the glass, before falling away entirely and dropping onto the floor. On the other side of the window, several people in the crowd had seen exactly what had just happened; some of them turned away, while others stared in stunned silence. Fortunately nobody fainted or screamed.

"I guess that made the decision for us," Toby pointed out, watching as the eyeball rolled to a stop on the floor. "Take photos, bag it up and... we'll let Sheriff Tench decide what to do with it, I guess. If he can drag himself away from the hospital." He took another pause, before turning to see several colleagues checking the scene round the corner. "Okay, show me what we've got."

***

"This is... intense."

"That's not quite the word I'd use," Sheila admitted, as they stood looking down at what remained of Wendy's body. "Do you know what it reminds me of? It reminds me of when you swat a fly and it sort of... leaks and bursts, and there are bits of goo coming out in little shiny blobs and..."

Her voice trailed off as she realized that everyone was looking at her.

"I'm sorry," she added, "that might have been inappropriate to say."

"No, you've got a point," Toby said, clearly struggling a little to control his sense of nausea as he looked down at Wendy's corpse. "Someone really went to town on her, didn't they? It looks like she's been bitten, and beaten, and in places almost... ripped apart by someone's bare hands. The fury that would have to be involved, to drive someone to do that, is almost impossible to imagine."

"Do you think it's the same person who attacked Tommy?"

"If it isn't, it's a pretty big coincidence," he suggested, "although I thought I overheard someone at the station saying Sheriff Tench tracked that guy down and saw him fall off a cliff or something."

"Off a cliff?"

They both paused for a moment.

"Then who did this?" she continued. "A friend of the first killer?"

Crouching down, Toby forced himself to look more closely at what was left of Wendy's face. Both her eyes had been ripped out, and he couldn't help thinking that eyes certainly seemed to be a common theme in everything that had been happening of late. He'd never really fancied himself as much of a detective, but now he wondered why people were having their eyes ripped out all over the town. For the first time in his life, he felt the little cogs turning in his mind as he tried to put all the pieces together. Finally an answer bubbled to the surface of his thoughts, and he felt slightly pleased with himself for having managed to think like the detectives on television.

"She's on display," he whispered.

"What did you mean?" Sheila asked.

"Look at the way we've found her," he continued, glancing around at all the dismembered body parts and all the smeared blood. "It's not just that the killer made no effort to hide her. I think he actually wanted us to see all of this because he's... I think he's proud of what he did."

"Then what -"

"No, not proud," he added. "That's the wrong word. He wants to show us what he's capable of doing."

"He wants to show us that he can kill someone?"

"He wants to show us that he can kill someone in such a brutal way," he said, getting to his feet again and taking a step back. "He wants to show us that he's not shy about doing it. He wants to show us that he's strong."

Looking up, he saw that the security cameras had been ripped out.

"He doesn't want to let us see too much," he added, "but he sure as hell wants to make us realize that he did this and that..."

His voice trailed off yet again as he tried to understand.

"And that he can do it again," he added finally.

"Again?"

"This is a demonstration of a threat," he told her. "It's a warning. I think he wants something, and this is his way of showing us what'll happen if he doesn't get it."

"O... kay," Sheila said cautiously, struggling to keep up with his line of reasoning. "There's no note, though. Why wouldn't he let us know exactly what's he's after?"

"He must think that it's obvious. That only an idiot wouldn't understand."

He paused, and then they looked at each other with painfully befuddled expressions.

"Beats me," Sheila said finally, shrugging her shoulders, "but I really don't like the idea of some maniac running around the town and ripping out eyes." She looked toward the far window, and she could see that a couple of her colleagues were having to force the crowd to remain behind the tape.

"There's something going on in Sobolton, something big, and we can't hide it from people forever."

"I'm sure Sheriff Tench will know what to do," Toby replied, although his voice contained a mocking tone of sarcasm.

"*Are* you sure?" She turned to him. "Because it seems to me that Sheriff Tench hasn't really known what to do since he got here. I mean, he's not here right now, is he? Why not? What's so important at the hospital that he doesn't have time to come to the diner where a woman's been horribly murdered and mutilated? Do you remember when we were out at the pylon a while ago? Sheriff Tench barely had that situation under control. Now apparently he can't be here because whatever's going on at the hospital matters more to him."

"It's Little Miss Dead," Toby replied darkly.

"The poor kid who got murdered? The one whose killer he can't even find?"

"Keep your voice down," Toby said, taking her by the arm and leading her around the counter so that they wouldn't be overheard by the others. "I heard Carolyn talking," he continued, lowering his voice to a conspiratorial hush. "Little Miss Dead... isn't Little Miss Dead anymore."

"I don't get it."

"She's Little Miss Alive."

"How -"

Stopping herself just in time, Sheila tried to comprehend everything she'd just heard.

"Exactly," Toby continued. "Somehow she's alive now, so I guess there's no killer to catch. Or if there is, the killing didn't exactly stick, but you and I both know that a full autopsy was carried out on her. And Robert Law might not be the best guy in the world, but I'm pretty sure he knows whether someone's dead or not." He looked past her, watching the crowd outside for a few seconds. "So if you're worried about people panicking, then I've got some news for you. I think panicking might actually be a pretty good idea."

"This is getting too big," she replied, with fear in her eyes. "We need outside help. And if Sheriff Tench won't call for it, then... we're going to have to do it ourselves."

"You mean get our hands dirty?" He thought about that prospect for a moment. "Hell, what not?" he added finally. "After all, I seem to be on a roll."

CHAPTER NINE

Hellevoetsluis, Holland – 1688...

"LOOK AT THEM," CLARA whispered, standing with her husband Henry on a hill overlooking the bustling Dutch port. Even at night, the lights on all the ships blazed with dazzling intensity. "How many of them do you think there are?"

"Enough, hopefully," Henry replied, with a tone of great seriousness in his voice. "Enough to smash the popish forces they'll meet when they arrive in England, at least."

"The weather is not in their favor."

"The weather will change its mind."

"But -"

"Everyone is praying for that," he continued. "When I walked through the city earlier, all the churches were full. People are beseeching the Lord to make the conditions perfect. Once they reach England, I am quite sure that Prince William and his forces will make short work of seizing the English crown and casting that devilish buffoon King James into some dark pit somewhere. Hopefully he will rot away and be quickly forgotten."

"And then our homeland will be free again?"

"I'm sure there will be those who'll fight back and try to restore the vile king," he suggested, "but they shall not endure, not when Prince William has right on his side. God will see that he emerges victorious."

"So..."

Clara thought for a moment. As a rule she tended not to challenge or contradict her husband in any manner, yet she couldn't help but wonder whether he'd overlooked one rather important element of the situation. Having wrestled with the question for some time, she knew that she simply had to bring this development to his attention. After all, she had family back in England and she hadn't entirely given up hope of one day seeing them again.

"My love," she continued cautiously, "it is two years now since we left Plymouth. I had thought that we would not still be here in Holland all this time later."

"Mr. Humford's men are still making the necessary arrangements," Henry replied. "I always told you that this would not be the work of a moment."

"Of a moment, no," she agreed, "but it's difficult not to wonder whether we shall ever set sail." She paused, worried that she should say no more, that she should keep all further fears to herself. "Indeed," she added, "one is tempted to wonder whether this is some kind of... sign."

"What kind of sign?"

"From... above?"

"Above?"

"What if the Lord doesn't want us to set sail for the Americas at all?" she asked, finally letting her fears spill out. "What if this is His way of showing us that we should turn back and return to the land of our birth?" With tears in her eyes, she waited for her husband to reply, and her own view on the matter was evident: she desperately wanted to go back to England. "I've heard stories about the Americas, Henry. Horrible, terrifying stories about a wild and savage place. Why, I fear that there is nothing godly there at all."

"That is precisely why we must go," he countered. "To *take* such qualities with us and help them to spread across that vast place."

"But -"

"America," he added firmly, "must be civilized before it's too late. There is potential for that place to become truly awful if it's left untamed."

"But it's so dangerous," she continued. "Think of our daughters. Are we really going to unleash such an irreligious place upon them?"

"They are strong young women," he replied, still watching the boats that bobbed up and down on the dark water. "They will find their way, as we will find ours. I daresay they will find fine husbands, too, and eventually they'll start families of their own."

"I just want them to be happy," Clara added, reaching out and touching his arm as if she was on the verge of *demanding* a change to their plans. "Think on this, Henry. Think on it carefully. If Prince William is truly going to free our home and overthrow our enemies, then why do we need to flee at all? We can wait for them to be done, and then we can go back and get on with our lives. We shall be on the victorious side, so our fortunes will be much improved! Do not forget, also, that my mother is still in England."

"I have not forgotten that. We shall set sail for America as soon as possible."

"I just fear that we might be making a mistake, that in our haste to keep ourselves safe we might be making the most dreadful wrong move."

She waited, hoping against hope that she might have managed to persuade him. When he turned to her, however, she immediately saw the expression of determination in his eyes. In that moment, she understood that her husband's mind was not for changing and that he failed to see the merit in her argument.

"We've come this far," he told her, as voices cried out in the harbor and bells rang, signaling that the invasion fleet would soon set sail for England. "I'm sorry, Clara, but we're not going to turn back." Reaching down, he took hold of her hands and squeezed them tight. "Don't worry," he added. "I shall keep you, Belle and Mary safe. Always."

***

Two months later, the pale and closed-eyed faces of Clara, Belle and Mary Sobolton remained entirely still as the boat rocked and creaked on the ocean. After a moment, a gray cloth was drawn over the three women, covering their bodies from sight.

"Lord," Father Ebeneezer Peck said solemnly, standing nearby on the boat's deck, "we commend the souls of these three of your children to your care, and we commend their earthly remains to the depths of your ocean, and we beseech thee to look over them as you would your own children, and take them into your eternal love and care.

Amen."

"Amen," several other travelers murmured nearby.

"We know that they suffered greatly," Father Peck continued, "but we also know that you have your reasons. It is not our place to question why such suffering must exist in this world, only to endure it and to praise all of your creations. For thy wisdom is greater than any wisdom that could ever exist in our minds, and we all hold hope that we shall be reunited when we reach your loving embrace."

"Amen," came the reply from the gathered crowd once more.

In his right hand, Father Peck was holding a small fragment of bone, attached to the end of a glistening gold chain. This piece of bone had been handed down by generation after generation, ever since it had been cracked away from the skull of the martyr Saint Thomas Becket in Canterbury Cathedral five centuries earlier.

"And although we shall soon venture into a strange new world," Father Peck added, as he watched the piece of bone swinging from the chain, "we are warmed and comforted by the certain knowledge that we take you with us wherever we might go. O Lord, watch over us and keep us safe in our endeavors, so that we can spread your word to all we might meet. Amen."

"Amen."

Staring with tear-stained eyes that were now red raw from crying, Henry Sobolton barely heard the priest's words at all. Instead he was looking at the three bodies that lay beneath the fabric, and he couldn't help replaying their final moments over and over again. A sickness had spread through the vessel in recent days, striking down men, women and children with seeming abandon. Two dozen had died, mostly passengers, and now his wife and daughters were part of their dreaded number.

"You shall not die," he remembered telling Clara. "I shall not permit it."

"I fear it is not in your gift to permit or deny such matters," she'd groaned weakly. "If this is what the Lord wants of me, and of our dear children, then we must accept our fates."

"You shall merely sleep," he'd insisted. "When you wake up, we shall be in the new world."

Those words sounded so hollow now – almost mocking – as they went round and round in his head. Having spent so much time promising his wife and daughters that they would be fine, and that they would surely make a swift recovery, he now felt like the most terrible and pathetic liar.

"Let us do it, then," Father Peck continued, taking a step back as he made the sign of the cross against his chest. "Let us consign the bodies of these three innocents to the ocean."

Three men made their way forward and began to lift the wooden supports beneath the bodies. The supports seemed to stick for a moment, but finally the three dead women slid down and fell from the side of the boat, crashing down together into the rough waves below.

"No!" Henry shouted, suddenly rushing forward and clambering up onto the side of the ship, ready to jump after them. "Wait!"

"Stop him!" Father Peck called out, and three other men quickly grabbed Henry's arms and pulled him back down. "Hold him, so that he cannot fall victim to his own weakness!"

"I want to go with them!" Henry sobbed. "Why am I alive and healthy, while they are dead?"

"Nobody knows the cause of this sickness," Father Peck reminded him. "It seems to ravage one and spare the other, with no order other than the Lord's will."

"Why would the Lord murder my daughters?" Henry snarled, turning to him.

"One must be careful with one's choice of words," Father Peck replied, looking down as if he couldn't quite bring himself to meet Henry's gaze. "There is nothing to be gained from being... excessive."

"I swore to protect them!" Henry hissed, as the men continued to hold him back. "I gave them my word, and now they're down there in the depths of the Atlantic where... they'll be eaten by fish! What kind of grave is this for them? I could not even bury them in hallowed ground!"

"One must not think of such things," Father Peck said, still with an extremely calm and untroubled demeanor. "The Lord means for all of this to happen. It is not for us to question his ways, for He sees and understands all. You must be strong, Mr. Sobolton, and not allow yourself to wallow in foolish emotions such as grief and self-pity. If He has seen fit to take your family from you, then it must be because He has some other task for you, one that he believes you can better accompany if you are unburdened by such ties."

"Do you really believe that?" Henry asked, shocked by the priest's callous suggestion.

"I know it to be true," Father Peck said firmly. "You must recall, the truth has no duty to make itself palatable to any of us. What it is, it is. And what shall be, shall be. Amen."

"Amen," several other men agreed.

Staring at the waves, Henry thought about his family's bodies sinking down through the cold darkness and eventually bumping to a rest at the bottom of the ocean. He thought about all the fish and other creatures that would soon find them, that would waste no time in eating through their flesh. Soon there would be nothing left but bones, and even these would over time become worn smooth by the movement of the water. He wanted nothing more than to go down there and join them, to gather up their bodies and hold them tight, to make them realize that they weren't alone and that he hadn't abandoned them at all, not even in death.

After a few more seconds, however, he began to pull back from the edge, and the men around him loosened their grips in turn.

"We are three days out from the new world," one of the others pointed as, as the ship crashed through some slightly stronger waves. "Perhaps four. I don't know about the rest of you, but I for one can't wait to get off this vessel and never see the wretched thing again. I want to feel nothing but dry land beneath my feet for the rest of my life."

The men were talking to each other as they walked away, leaving Henry standing near the railing. He was still watching the waves, but all thoughts of jumping into the ocean had left him now. Instead he felt utterly drained of all feeling and he wanted simply to stop thinking, and to stop feeling, and to simply stop existing at all. Throwing himself into the ocean, he knew, would achieve all of that in a manner, but now he had a better idea. He turned and looked toward the west, and he thought of the vast new world waiting for him, and he told himself that instead he was going to throw himself into that world. Anything else, he knew now, would be the ultimate betrayal of his dead family.

"Their deaths," he whispered somberly, "shall not be in vain."

"Nor shall the deaths of any of the Lord's children," Father Peck said, having lingered nearby. He was holding the relic of Saint Thomas Becket and turning it between his fingertips. "That is how it has always been, and how it shall always be. We are here, after all, merely to do the Lord's work."

CHAPTER TEN

Sobolton, USA – Today...

THE HOSPITAL BED CREAKED slightly as a pair of scratched, bloodied bare feet slowly lowered down onto the polished floor.

Sitting on the side of the bed, with the pair of scissors in her left hand, Lisa watched the door intently. She'd already begun to work out the routine of the ward, and she felt fairly sure that the various staff-members from the desk had just headed off to check on someone at the other end of the corridor. She knew she didn't have long, so she quickly made her way to the door and looked out. She could hear voices, but there was no sign of anyone. Having already carefully disabled the monitors and removed the various wires attached to her body, she slipped out of the room and scurried almost silently through to the office behind the main desk.

Once she was in there, she took a moment to figure out her surroundings. She spotted a white medical coat hanging from a hook, so she grabbed that and put it on. She saw some shoes too – loafers, actually – and she quickly discovered that they more or less fit her feet. Turning, she looked around the room again, trying to find anything that might be useful, and finally she saw a mirror above a sink in the corner. She walked over and looked at her own reflection, and in that moment she froze.

"I'm old," she whispered, reaching up and touching her face.

For a moment, she could only stare in horror at the woman in the mirror. She almost didn't recognize herself; she'd lost so much weight over the twenty years, and her hair had become a graying mess, and even her eyes seemed different somehow. She felt an instinctive sense of sorrow as she realized just how much she'd changed while she was out there in the forest; she'd known that time was passing, of course, but it was only now that she truly registered just how much of her life had been stolen.

"I'm old," she said again, this time with more of a shocked but resigned tone. "I'm so old."

Stepping back, she quickly reminded herself that there would be time for self-pity later. Her mind was racing and she knew that she couldn't afford to get caught; after all, she felt very weak and she figured that any security guard would be able to restrain her without even breaking a sweat. Instead, she tried to focus on the task at hand, and as she edged to the opposite door and pulled it open, she found herself looking out into a different corridor. She could hear voices in the distance, and her heart was pounding as she realized that someone would find her empty bed at any moment.

"Where are you?" she whispered, trying to come up with a better plan. "Eloise, where the hell have they taken you?"

***

"There's been a call about something happening at the diner in town," John said as he led Eloise and Robert away from the front of the hospital. "I have to get down there and check it out."

"Is anyone hurt?" Robert asked.

Reaching the police cruiser that was waiting to pick him up, John turned to Robert and almost began to explain, before remembering that Eloise was listening and that she might be horrified.

"I'll deal with that," he said cautiously. "Bob, I know this is a huge thing to ask, but I need someone to keep an eye on the girl for a few hours."

"Of course."

"I don't think I need to tell you that she needs to be kept out of harm's way."

"Absolutely," Robert replied, "but... John, the monster that attacked Tommy -"

"He's dead," John said firmly. "I think so, at least. To be honest, with the way things are going lately, I don't think we can be sure about anything. But I saw him fall, and I'm going to send a team out to retrieve his body."

"Whose body?" Eloise asked.

"That's nothing for you to be concerned about," John told her, forcing a smile as he glanced at her, then turning away in the hope that she might not hear the rest of the conversation. "I also need to get some people out to the cabin," he continued, lowering his voice a little. "There are so many active parts of this investigation right now, and I'm still trying to work out exactly how they all fit together." He leaned a little closer. "I'm worried about the girl," he added, "so can you do one thing for me? Take her to the station and keep her there. Keep her safe. I don't care if you have to lock her in a cell. If that's what it takes, then do it."

"You think someone's after her?"

"Until Lisa Sondnes wakes up, we won't know anything for certain, but we have to assume that she's a target. Robert, I'm not asking you to put yourself in danger, I just need you to get her to the station. Whoever you find, tell them the situation and make sure that they do whatever it takes to look after her. I won't be long, I'll catch up to you soon." He turned to open the cruiser's door. "I just -"

Suddenly his knees buckled. Reaching out, he tried to keep himself up, but he let out a gasp of pain as he leaned against the side of the cruiser.

"John!" Robert gasped, hurrying over and grabbing him by the arm, keeping him from toppling over entirely. "What is it?"

"Nothing!" John hissed, but he was clearly in agony and after a moment he reached down and put a hand on his chest. "It's nothing!" he stammered. "Just... from last night..."

After a few more seconds, the pain began to pass. Clearly still uncomfortable, John waited a moment longer before managing to get back up. He pushed Robert's hand away and took a deep breath, and then he tried to laugh as he rubbed his chest a little.

"It's nothing," he continued, before glancing at Robert. "Don't give me that look, Bob. I'm fine."

"Sure, because people who are fine almost collapse in hospital parking lots after not sleeping all night."

"I don't need this right now, Bob."

"And your hands aren't exactly getting any better," Robert added skeptically. "John, you're not going to do anyone any favors if you run yourself into the ground. It's better to rest, take care of yourself for a few hours while you let other people put in the work, and then you can come back refreshed and ready to do business."

"I can't do that right now."

"Why not?"

"Because the whole damn town needs me!" John hissed. "That's why! I have to prove to them all that I can keep Sobolton safe!"

He waited for an answer, but after a moment he turned to see that Eloise was staring at him with a puzzled expression.

"Are you really the sheriff?" she asked.

"Don't start," John muttered, before pulling the cruiser's door open. "I'll meet you both at the station in an hour or two. When I get there, we'll go through everything we need to do next and we'll set out a clear plan of action." He paused, painfully aware that he needed to make Eloise feel better but not really sure how to go about doing that. After a moment he stepped over and, after some brief hesitance, he reached out and put a hand on her shoulder. "Young lady," he continued, "let me assure you that we're all doing everything in our power not only to keep you safe, but also to make sure that your mother is well looked after. We're putting all our effort into this task and you mustn't doubt for even one second that we're going to sort everything out."

He paused, before patting her on the

shoulder and climbing into the cruiser.

"Bob, I'll see you at the station."

Robert and Eloise stepped back and watched as the cruiser drove away. As the vehicle rounded the corner and disappeared from sight, Eloise furrowed her brow slightly.

"Why is he so weird?" she asked finally.

"I've been asking myself that question for a while," Robert admitted with a sigh, before looking down at her. "Let's do as he said, and get to the station. But on the way, do you want to stop and get pancakes? Because I know I do."

"Okay," she said, nodding gently, but she still seemed confused. "But... what's a pancake?"

"Kid," he replied, leading her toward his car at the far end of the parking lot, "I'm truly jealous. I'd give anything to be able to experience the joy of my very first pancake all over again. But you'd probably better let me choose the toppings."

"Okay," she said, before pausing for a moment. "What's a topping?"

CHAPTER ELEVEN

The New World – 1698...

DRIVING SNOW BLASTED THROUGH the air, rustling the nearby trees that stood at the edge of a vast forest. The sky was a huge blanket of white, and the entire land in this area appeared entirely untouched save for a set of footsteps that had been left in the snow by a dark figure pushing through the blizzard.

Stopping for a moment, Henry Sobolton lowered the rough scrap of fabric he'd been using to cover his face. A scar ran down past his left eye now, the result of a drunken brawl with some idiot a few years earlier. Henry had been in the Americas for a decade now, but he'd long since left other people behind. Sick and tired of dealing with all the fools he'd met, he'd resolved to strike out on his own, venturing beyond the colonies and forging his own path through the wild untamed wilderness that remained unmapped and unknown, at least to any new arrival.

Now, however, Henry was starting to think that he might have gone too far, that he might perhaps have ventured so starkly beyond the edge of civilization that he was in a place where nobody and nothing could live. He'd certainly seen no sign of life for several days now, and his meager rations were getting dangerously low. He knew that if he was unable to find at least a few scraps soon, he would surely be dead by the end of the week.

As if to emphasize that point, his stomach scratched and rumbled, begging to be filled by something; by anything, really, even bark from the trees.

Setting off again, Henry figured that there was no point trying to turn back. He would most certainly die before he reached the last town he'd visited, so he could only force his way through the snow and hope that he might find some shelter somewhere and perhaps even something to eat. His ankles were burning thanks to the effort required to push through so much snow, but he kept going until finally he disappeared into the distance, fading into the blizzard's vast white wall.

***

A few hours later, crawling through the snow on his hands and feet, Henry finally managed to throw himself into a small space beneath various branches that had formed a crude shelter. He pulled himself further inside, and then he turned to look back out as more and more snow continued to fall.

The shelter, such as it was, seemed to have been formed by several falling branches. Leaning out and looking up, Henry saw the trees rising up high all around. Although the chance of these particular branches falling and landing in this particular manner seemed low, he was in no mood to question what seemed in that instant to be a moment of profound relief. Pulling back into his little makeshift sanctuary, shivering as he felt patches of cold water melting through his clothes, he began to wonder just how long he should spend undercover.

Too long, he knew, and he'd simply freeze to death in this very spot.

"I can't give up," he whispered, trying to boost his own flagging morale. "I'm doing this for..."

In his mind's eye, he once again saw the three bodies falling off the side of the ship and crashing down into the waves. He thought, too, of how cold they must have been once they reached the bottom of the ocean, and he told himself that – compared to such horrors – he really had no cause for complaint. He had failed his beautiful, caring wife and his two innocent daughters, and now he had to pay for that sin. Every gram of pain was deserved, and he supposed that the only reason to keep living was so that he could feel more and more agony, so that he could continue to atone for the horrors he'd inflicted on those who'd relied upon him the most.

Staring straight ahead for a moment, he saw more snow falling, but he also began to spot a vague darkness somewhere in the distance. He blinked a couple of times, convinced that he must be mistaken, but slowly the darkness was starting to resolve and become three blurry figures. Already he knew, from their heights alone, exactly who he was seeing: the ghosts of his dead family had followed him from the ocean and had now arrived in the desolate snowy wastelands of the new world.

"Clara," he stammered, squinting in an effort to see her better. "Is that you?"

Shifting until he was on his knees, he watched as the figures slowly began to make their way closer. He felt the dread tightening and solidifying in his chest as the figures began to emerge from the snowstorm. They were only a hundred feet or so away now, close enough to see properly in normal conditions, but with snow still swirling all around he could barely make them out at all.

Yet it was them.

Of that, he had no doubt.

"I'm sorry," he continued, as he began to taste blood at the back of his throat. "We should never have left for this awful place. You were right, Clara. By now, Prince William will surely have taken the throne of England, and we could be back there living our old lives. Instead..."

His voice trailed off for a few seconds as the figures continued to advance.

"Instead I insisted on bringing us out here, and my foolish notions led to your deaths."

He clutched his hands together in a sort of mock prayer, although he couldn't quite bring himself to *actually* pray. Why, he wondered, would the Lord ever listen to a man who had created so much misery?

"I cannot defend myself," he added. "We all know that. There is no absolution for a man such as myself. I can only hope that your souls will be delivered to paradise, even as mine must burn in the deepest pits of Hell."

As he waited for an answer, the snowstorm briefly cleared for just a fraction of a second, and in that moment Henry saw the faces of his wife and daughters.

He let out a gasp as he found himself staring

at their dead, partially hollow eyes. Having expected to see them as they were in life, now he found himself instead seeing them as three dead, almost rotten corpses standing tall in the American wilderness. Their skin had been eaten away in places, no doubt by monstrous creatures of the deep, exposing patches of bare bone. Slowly, Henry began to realize that he was seeing his family as they must be now, down in the depths of the ocean with marine animals eating through their flesh and making homes in their bones. Sure enough, he spotted a foul creature moving in the empty socket of his wife's left eye.

"The sea was no hallowed grave," he sobbed, with tears running down his face. "That foolish priest barely even knew the right words to say. Are you doomed to forever haunt this world, unable to move on to the next? Did I fail you yet again, even after you had died?"

The figures were still making their way closer, and finally Henry found himself staring up at them. Already he could feel the hatred emanating from their bodies, and he wanted to find some way to show them that he was sorry. He slowly got to his feet, barely able to stand now on faltering legs that seemed set to crumble at any moment. Looking at his daughters, he saw that their faces were barely recognizable; latticed holes had been gnawed into their cheeks, allowing all sorts of tiny worms and other creatures to burrow deeper, and the rags of the girls' dresses now hung on skeletal remains that were barely held together by thin scraps of meat.

Turning to Clara, Henry felt his heart break as he saw some kind of crustacean staring back at him from her hollowed cheek. After a moment Clara began to open her mouth, causing her exposed jawbone to click. She tried to say something, but instead a torrent of seawater and small mollusks dribbled from her lips and fell down her chin, while the foulest stench of death began to fill the air.

"Do what you will with me," Henry said, as more and more tears ran from his eyes. "Take me to the gates of Hell, if that is your intent. I shall not argue, nor shall I attempt to disprove my sins, for I know what I am. I am a bad man, a foolish man, a vain man and a failed man. For I failed the most important people in my life. I failed my family."

He waited, but Clara – or what remained of Clara – merely stared back at him.

"Do it!" he screamed, suddenly losing all control and raising his voice so that it echoed out across the vast wilderness. "End it now! Take me to Hell!"

AMY CROSS

CHAPTER TWELVE

Sobolton, USA – Today...

"IS IT HIM?" TOBY asked, watching as John crouched in front of Wendy's body and inspected the horrific mess. "It's him, right? This is the same bastard who did all that awful stuff to Tommy."

John peered more closely at the cracked and broken side of Wendy's eyeless face. He blinked a couple of times, observing the chaotic damage, and then finally he got to his feet.

"No."

"No?"

"No, I don't think it is," he continued, before turning to Toby and Sheila. "What happened to Tommy was more calculated. More focused. This is more furious. Whoever killed this woman, I think they..."

He paused as he tried to find the right words.

"I think they enjoyed it."

"Great," Sheila said, "so now you think we've got two murderous psychos on the loose?"

"I wouldn't say that, necessarily," John replied. "I need a team of two or three to head out past Henge Cliff. I'll mark the precise location on a map, although it might be a little vague. I need them to search for a body in the river, and it might have washed a short distance downstream. However, I'm fairly certain that the individual who attacked Tommy is now dead."

"But you're not *sure*," Toby said skeptically.

"I want to see a body," John said firmly.

"I don't want to see another body ever again," Sheila whispered, unable to stop staring down at Wendy's corpse.

"Let's sort out this scene," John continued, "and then I need another team to come with me out to the forest."

"To look for the body in the river?"

"No, to turn a cabin upside down and find out what we can about the place," John replied. "I'm sorry, but we need all hands on deck, so you're going to have to bring in people even if they've got time off. I'll be leading the team out to the cabin myself, but I'll be available over the radio at all times. People, I don't need to tell you how much is riding on this investigation. The safety of the entire town is at stake."

"We know that," Toby said firmly. "Meanwhile, what are you going to do about *them*?"

He nodded toward the window. Turning, John saw that the crowd was still gathered outside, and that if anything a few more onlookers had shown up to try to see what was happening. Covers had been raised to block parts of the scene, but John already knew that he was going to have to address the public soon.

"I'll call a meeting later," he said finally. "For now, let's concentrate on the tasks at hand. Before I start talking to everyone, I need to have a little more to say about what's actually going on."

***

"That?" Al said, turning to look at the framed photo that stood at the far end of the bar in McGinty's. "Oh, that's Sheryl. Sheryl Digger. She's a girl who worked here a while back, but..."

He paused as he looked at Sheryl's smiling face.

"Well, something bad happened," he continued, before turning to the man who'd asked about her just a moment earlier. "Then again, this is Sobolton," he added, rolling his eyes. "When *doesn't* something bad happen round these parts?"

He paused again, as if lost in thought.

"It's funny," he continued. "Sometimes I wonder just how much craziness this town can put up with. It's like we're cursed or something, like maybe someone did something really bad a long time ago, and now the entire town has to deal with the consequences. I'm not some kind of nut, and I usually keep these thoughts to myself, but they play on my mind from time to time and -"

He stopped himself just in time, before managing an exasperated – and slightly embarrassed – laugh.

"You know what?" he asked. "I don't know why I'm even telling you all of this."

"That's alright," the man on the stool by the window said, staring back at him with his one good eye. The other eye was covered by a black patch. "I tend to have that effect on people."

"So are you just passing through?" Al asked, getting back to his routine of polishing glasses. "Are you new around here?"

"A little of both," the man murmured, before turning and looking out the window again. From his vantage point, he could just about make out the entrance to the sheriff's station in the distance, and that was no coincidence. He squinted for a moment, watching as two women walked past. "I've got some family business to take care of."

"You've picked a ripe old day for it," Al replied. "There's some nasty business at the diner, from what I've heard. There are some pretty horrible rumors going round town about what might have happened over there."

"I bet there are," the man purred.

"So you've got family here, huh?" Al continued. "Anyone I might know?"

"I doubt that very much," the man replied.

"I know most people round these parts," Al told him. "In my line of business, I come into contact with pretty much everyone. The drunks, the layabouts, the hard-working bastards who need a drink so they can let off steam. They all come by here. Not a lot happens in this town that I don't hear about."

"Is that right?" the man asked gruffly, still watching the sheriff's station.

"Things have been kinda strange lately," Al explained. "Stranger than normal. I don't know if you heard, but a little girl was found dead in the ice out at Drifter's Lake."

"Yes," the man said darkly, "I heard."

"Then there was some business out at Wentworth Stone's mansion," Al continued. "I don't think *anyone* quite knows what that was all about. Some nonsense about swans, apparently, although I admit that sounds pretty odd. I must have misunderstood."

The man at the window allowed himself a faint smile.

"Then Sheriff Hicks died," Al added. "Sorry, *former* Sheriff Hicks. You know, I still can't quite get used to that fact. He used to come in here a lot and shoot the breeze. Sure, he wasn't always popular and I'm sure he... cut a few corners, but he got things done. I'm not sure I have quite such a good opinion of his replacement." He took a moment to scratch away a particularly stubborn mark on one of the glasses. "I heard his end wasn't too nice," he said with a sigh. "There are rumors he got attacked by wolves."

"Yes," the man at the window, and now his smile grew. "I remember."

"Then there was a big power cut and all sorts of stuff went down, and apparently one of the guys at the station got horribly attacked by some transient psycho, so I guess you could say that Sobolton's seen more than its fair share of drama lately. Even by our usual high standards. Then there was what happened to Sheryl a few years back, and all that weird stuff with the ice cream store. You know, when it's all laid out like that, I can't help but wonder how anyone survives in this place. You never know what's coming next. I wouldn't be at all surprised if the heavens crashed down one day."

The man at the window opened his mouth to reply, but in that moment he spotted a car parking near the sheriff's station. His senses began to tingle, and sure enough he saw an older man stepping out of the vehicle, followed by Eloise.

"There you are," he whispered, before downing his drink and getting to his feet.

"You off?" Al asked.

"I am," the man replied, heading to the door. "Thank you kindly for your hospitality. You have a very nice little place here."

"Good luck with the folks."

"Thank you, but I don't think I need luck." He pulled the door open and stepped outside, just in time to see Robert Law and Eloise heading into the sheriff's station. "Luck's just an excuse people use when they can't get the job done."

"I didn't catch your name," Al called after him.

"No, you didn't," the man replied, stopping for a moment with the door still open, then turning to look back through at Al. "I have a slightly odd name, actually. My father gave the normal name to one of my brothers, to the one he thought was going to be important one day. So I got the weird name, because I don't really matter. My father named me after one of his favorite historical figures." He paused, and now his smile really grew. "My name's Saint Thomas, and I truly try to live up to that title. It can be hard, though. Sometimes, I admit, I fall short." He paused again. "*Very* short."

AMY CROSS

CHAPTER THIRTEEN

The New World – 1698...

HE WAS WOKEN BY the sound of treetops rustling nearby.

Opening his eyes, blinking in an attempt to see properly, Henry Sobolton found himself on his side in the small shelter. He blinked again, and he saw now that the snow had stopped falling, although plenty of the wretched white stuff remained on the ground all around. As he began to sit up, he felt every bone in his body crying out from stiffness, but for a moment he was scarcely able to remember where he was, or how he'd ended up there, or even his own name.

Looking out across the wilderness, he saw vast swathes of snow-topped forest covering what seemed to be some wildly undulating land. Whereas on the previous day he'd heard the sound of snow falling, and his own ragged breath, now he was astonished by the utter silence of a scene that he could only describe as beautiful. He saw his own half-buried steps in the snow, but after a moment he spotted what appeared to be a second – and clearer – set of tracks leading off in a different direction. Telling himself that he must be mistaken, that he must have caused those tracks as well, he pulled back a little, and in that moment he bumped against something that had been left hanging from part of the shelter.

He turned, and to his astonishment he saw several skinned rabbits hanging from pieces of twine.

Reaching out, barely able to believe this development, he pulled one of the rabbits closer. It wasn't frozen, which suggested that it hadn't been out for long, but the meat appeared to be good and he began to realize that it had been cooked, too. He turned the rabbit around, in awe at the sight of such food, and he realized that he couldn't remember a time when he'd been close to such good meat. Already the claws in his belly were waking, scratching at the sides and begging for their hunger to be sated, and finally Henry could no longer help himself.

Pulling the rabbit closer, he bit deep into its

side. As he began to chew, he tasted the wonderful flavors of the meat, which he realized now had been slightly salted. He bit off some more, then more still, and he found himself unable to even slow down as he devoured the rabbit. Soon he was grinding his teeth on the bones, desperate for every fleck of meat, until finally he threw the carcass aside and pulled down the second rabbit. His stomach was filling now, although it had been empty for so long that the presence of food now brought a little pain. This wasn't enough to stop him, however, and he remained on his knees until he'd finished not only the first two rabbits but also the third.

Finally, seeing that he was finished, he tossed the third set of bones aside and got to his feet. He felt stronger now, almost renewed, as he looked once more around and found that the harsh landscape seemed less alien now. The night before, he'd felt as if he was surely about to die, yet now he felt so much more powerful. He briefly thought back to the previous night's visions of his wife and daughters, but he put those thoughts out of his mind as he realized that by some miracle he'd been saved. Telling himself that in his delirium he must have caught and killed those rabbits – and ignoring the problem of how they might have been cooked – he hauled his sack over his shoulders and set off away from the suspiciously well-built shelter.

***

Although the snow had stopped falling and a bright sun now burned in the sky, there was still far too much snow on the ground for progress to be easy. Nevertheless, over the next few hours Henry Sobolton made good progress, eventually passing through a section of the forest before emerging and finding himself standing on the shore of what appeared to be a large and partially-frozen lake.

A few pieces of ice drifted past on sections where the water was still free.

"This is a fine place," Henry said out loud, and he wondered if he was the first man *ever* to speak in such a strange place. "A man could do something with land like this."

As he watched the lake's distant shores, he felt his mind filling with all sorts of strange plans and ideas. This was exactly the kind of virgin, unspoiled world that had filled his wildest dreams. When he'd been sitting with his family back in England, trying to encourage them as he planned their journey to the new world, this was *precisely* the kind of landscape that he'd been trying to make them imagine. There was no sign of anyone else in this place, suggesting that there was little danger of other men arriving and getting in his way.

This was a new land.

This was...

"Soboltonland," he whispered, imagining that he could establish a whole kingdom of his own. Finally a smile broke across his lips, although this was quickly tempered by the thought of so much hard work ahead.

Yet...

Hard work did not frighten Henry Sobolton. Indeed, in some manner that he didn't fully understand, the prospect of hard work actually made him feel stronger, as if his muscles were already rising to meet the challenge.

"I name this place Soboltonland," he pronounced, raising his voice a little. "I claim it in the name of the rightful king of England, King William, and in his honor I shall work the land and make it more hospitable. I shall see what lurks beneath the snow, and I shall make a place that is free of vile persecution."

His mind was racing now with so many possibilities. Soboltonland, he quickly decided, would be a place where the petty sectarian arguments of the old world would be left far behind. There would be no popery, that much was certain, but a church would have to be constructed. He would build himself a humble dwelling, and he would learn to get the best out of the land. In time, he would be willing to admit others into his kingdom, but only on the condition that they must abide by his rules. Any man who arrived and tried to change things would quickly find himself cast out again, back into the wilderness, because -

"This is my land," he said, dropping his sack onto the ground and then stepping over to the edge of the lake. Kneeling, he dipped his fingers into the cold water. "This is my world," he continued, looking out across the lake. "It is everything I have ever dreamed of, and it is far removed from the grubby streets of London. I only wish -"

Hearing a branch snapping, he froze for a moment. He wanted to turn and look over his shoulder, but for a moment he was too scared by the thought that he might again see his family. Remembering the awful sight of their faces in his vision, he finally forced himself to look back; to his utmost relief, there was no sign of anyone at all, and instead he began to wonder about the creatures in the forest that might have caused such a sound. He knew he'd soon have to find a more reliable source of food, but he supposed that – as well as rabbits – there must be deer, and perhaps other animals that he had never seen before back in England.

In fact, as he continued to watch the treeline, he realized that this new world might hold many secrets, but he quickly told himself that he would master them all. The task would be great and onerous, but he felt absolutely certain that he was up to it and that eventually he would conquer this place from horizon to horizon. Already he had visions of a great town, a city even, that would rise from the wilderness. Soboltonland was going to become the perfect place for good, honest men and their families, and all evil and sin would be cast out.

"This is why I was saved," he said as he got to his feet, filled with a renewed sense of purpose. "This is why the Lord kept me in this world. He delivered me here so that I might fulfill his greatest dream of a sanctuary where good men can live their lives. It is in this task that I shall redeem my slovenly soul, and while I might never gain the forgiveness of my precious Clara and our daughters, I shall at least serve the Lord to the best of my ability."

Hurrying through the snow, he went back to the treeline and reached up, struggling for a moment before pulling down a large branch. He turned it around, and then he took a knife from his pocket and carved the name 'Soboltonland' into the wood. Once that was done, he hesitated for a moment, feeling a great sense of purpose, and then he drove one end of the branch into the ground before stepping back to see the result of his work.

"It is done," he said proudly. "Soboltonland is founded. Now let the real work begin."

CHAPTER FOURTEEN

Sobolton, USA – Today...

"SWEETHEART, YOU HAVE SUCH a lovely smile," Carolyn said, as she set her coffee cup down on the desk and stepped over to greet Eloise. "Now, what's a beautiful little lady such as yourself doing with us here today?"

"John wants me to... keep an eye on her," Robert said cautiously.

"What's that on the side of your face?" Carolyn asked, grabbing a tissue and wiping some smeared blueberry sauce from Eloise's chin.

"It's blueberry topping," Eloise said cautiously, "from on top of a pancake. That's the right word, isn't it?"

"It sure is," Robert replied. "We stopped to

get pancakes from the gas station opposite the cemetery. I know they're not exactly health food, but the poor kid didn't even know what a pancake was!"

"I do now," Eloise said, before thinking for a few seconds. "I really like them."

"I'm sure we can have lots of fun," Carolyn continued.

"You know who she is, right?" Robert replied.

"Should I?" Carolyn asked, looking over at him.

"Little Miss Dead," he mouthed silently.

"Huh?"

"Little Miss..." He said those words out loud, before mouthing the last part. "Dead."

"I'm not sure that I understand," Carolyn said cautiously. "Is this for some kind of... reconstruction? Are you gonna film her for the cameras and then show it to people, hoping to jog their memories?"

"It's nothing like that," Robert told her, before taking Eloise by the hand and leading her to the end of the corridor. "Honey, Eloise... do you see that second door there on the left?"

Eloise nodded.

"Why don't you go and wait for me in there? Sheriff Tench has some books, you can take a look through them. You know how to read, don't you?"

Eloise nodded again.

"Mommy taught me. She told me it was important."

"Then go and amuse yourself, and I'll be with you shortly."

He watched as she walked through to John's office, and then he turned to Carolyn.

"I'm losing my mind," he admitted. "I conducted a frickin' autopsy on that girl, and now she's up and walking around."

"That's not possible," Carolyn said cautiously.

"I know it's not possible, but you just saw her!" He sighed. "I took out her brain and weighed it. I had my hands in her guts. I cut her open, I took off the top of her skull and..."

His voice trailed off as he realized that he was still just as lost as ever.

"A Sobolton Special, huh?" Carolyn replied.

"I'm sorry?"

"That's what my friends always call it whenever Sobolton serves up one of its... stranger little quirky moments." She rolled her eyes. "Do you remember that ice cream place that opened in town a while back?"

"I don't recall an ice cream place."

"It wasn't there for very long," she told him. "It was called Sid's Ice Cream Parlor, and it sort of sprung up overnight and it was really bright and flashy. The strange part is, some people remember it really well, and others insist it was never there at all. But it *was* there, I know it was, because I actually got some ice cream from there. The girl who ran it was pretty weird, like she gave off the craziest vibes. I wasn't too surprised when the place just shut down one day, and the girl was never seen again. But it's one of those weird stories that Sobolton throws up sometimes, and I don't think that's ever going to change. Whatever's strange about Sobolton, whatever doesn't quite stack up... it's everywhere. It's in the soil. It's in the air. It's in the water. Without it, Sobolton wouldn't be Sobolton."

They stood in silence for a few seconds.

"I still don't remember an ice cream place," Robert said finally. "Are you sure you're not imagining things?"

"I don't think anyone could imagine an -"

Before she could finish, Carolyn heard a smashing sound, and she turned just in time to see that her coffee cup had fallen off the desk and had shattered against the floor. She stepped back as steaming hot coffee spilled out.

"Again?" she snapped angrily. "I swear I didn't put it on the edge this time! What's going on in this place?"

***

In John's office, Eloise made her way over to the set of shelves. She stopped to look at the books, and after a moment she pulled one out at random. She didn't really understand what it was about, but she liked the lurid cover and the garish images on what appeared to be some kind of horror novel.

A moment later, hearing a shuffling sound, she looked over her shoulder.

"Hello?" she said cautiously.

She waited, but the office was entirely empty. She looked at the chair behind the desk, but there was no sign of anyone, and then she looked at the equally bare sofa. Although she couldn't see anyone, in the back of her mind she couldn't shake the feeling that she was being watched. She turned to the windows, but all she saw outside was a set of bushes that for the most part obscured any further view.

Once she was confident that nobody was around, she looked back at the book in her hands. She began to flick through its pages, before closing the book again and taking another look at the cover.

"*The Haunting on Winchester Road,*" she read out loud, "by John Myers."

Opening the book yet again, she began to read a page at random, before suddenly letting out a gasp and spinning round. She still saw no-one, yet now she felt absolutely sure that she'd felt a hand briefly touch her shoulder. Stepping back, she bumped against the shelves, but her heart was pounding and she couldn't help constantly looking all around the room, convinced that at any second someone was going to step into view.

"Who are you?" she asked, and now her voice was filled with fear. "I know you're here. I want to see you."

Suddenly she heard laughter. She turned and looked over at the desk; the laughter ended abruptly, but after a few more seconds the office chair began to very slowly turn.

"Who are you?" she asked again, as the chair stopped once more.

She swallowed hard, and a moment later she heard the faint sound of invisible footsteps moving calmly across the room.

"Don't come near me!" she called out, stepping to the side and heading toward the door. At the same time, the book dropped from her hands and fell harmlessly to the floor. "I don't know who you are, but I don't want you to come anywhere near me! Leave me alone!"

She waited, but now the footsteps had come to a halt. Holding her breath, she told herself that so far everything about this place – about the office, about the building and even about the town itself – felt very wrong to her, as if this was a world in which she could never belong. A kind of haze hung in the air, a buzzy static that seemed to come from all the sockets on the walls and the light fittings high above. So far, other people seemed not to notice these things, and she'd kept quiet because she didn't want to upset anyone, but now a shudder passed through her chest as she realized that the static was getting stronger and stronger, almost as if -

A hand touched her shoulder from behind. Screaming, she spun around, only to find a bemused Carolyn and Robert standing in the open doorway.

"Hey there," Carolyn said cautiously, with a kind smile, "we heard you shouting. Is everything alright in here?"

Eloise turned and looked across the office again. She wanted to tell them about the strange things that had happened, but she was also keen to avoid making herself seem strange. She turned to Carolyn again, and after a few seconds she took a deep breath.

"Everything's fine," she said, before picking the book up from the floor. "This looks interesting. I thought I might read it."

"Let's go through to my office," Robert said, leading her out of the room and along the corridor. "It's a lot more comfortable than that hole John works in. I actually have a beanbag in my room. You probably don't know what a beanbag is, but you're gonna love it. I got it because it's good for my back..."

As Robert and Eloise disappeared around the corner, Carolyn took another quick look around John's empty office. Lately she'd been feeling distinctly uneasy, not only in this room but basically across the entire building. Finally she shut the door before going to grab a mop from one of the closets.

In John's office, a faint chuckle could now be heard. The office chair turned again, and – had anyone been standing in the exact right spot – they might have made out the face of Sheriff Joe Hicks reflected in one of the lamp covers.

CHAPTER FIFTEEN

Soboltonland, The New World – 1701...

A HAMMERING SOUND RANG out across the valley as Henry Sobolton, kneeling on a set of planks, continued his work. He had no nails, of course, but he'd developed his own methods of banging hand-carved wooden pegs into crude holes cut into the side of wood, and following this system he'd been able to construct a basic wooden home near the edge of the lake.

This summer had been warm, and the land was unrecognizable from the snowy world he'd first encountered when he'd arrived three years earlier.

Wincing, he leaned back and held his right hand up. A while earlier he'd caught his hand on some thick brambles, cutting a wound around the base of his thumb. He'd cleaned that wound to the best of his ability, but he was gradually becoming concerned by its refusal to heal; indeed, as he peered at the damage now, he saw that the skin around the wound's sides had become reddened and swollen, and that the flesh in the middle was discolored now with patches of yellow and green, even black.

He opened and closed his fist a few times, but even this simple movement now felt sore and strangely difficult.

Suddenly a howl rang out somewhere in the distance. Startled, Henry got to his feet and spun round. A row of skinned rabbits hung from a nearby post, waiting to be cooked, but Henry listened with fear as the howl continued and then faded to nothing. He looked out at the tops of the trees, and he quickly estimated that the strange noise had come from no more than a few miles away. His heart was racing as he tried to imagine what kind of creature could have made such a strange sound, but there was one from the old world that most certainly seemed to fit.

"Can there be wolves here in Soboltonland?" he whispered. "I'm not sure what the meat of a wolf tastes like, but I would be willing to try it."

He watched the trees. In truth, the forest extended for many miles all around, and Henry knew that the wolf – if it had even *been* a wolf – was probably so far away that it would never come close enough to cause trouble. Still, this was a timely reminder that even after three years Henry had not yet discovered everything that there was to know about his new home, and that danger might still arrive at any moment from any direction. Although he had taken measures to protect his fragile little settlement, Henry knew all too well that his position on the shore of the lake was rather too exposed. Indeed, for a while now he had been thinking that he should perhaps move to a safer location, perhaps somewhere within a few miles.

As he waited, he realized that the wolf was – for now, at least – silent again. Hopefully, he supposed, it had merely been passing through the area and soon it would be gone forever.

***

A few days later, after trekking through a familiar stretch of forest for a while, Henry Sobolton emerged from the shadows of the trees and stopped to look out across a remarkable sight.

For reasons that he couldn't possibly comprehend, a small valley did indeed exist in the midst of the forest, with far fewer trees than elsewhere. As he looked around at this almost miraculous vision, Henry was already starting to realize that *this* would be a much better place to build his kingdom. The lake was too open, too difficult to defend, but this small area just a short distance away seemed far more promising. In his mind's eye, he already imagined a thoroughfare passing through the middle, with small buildings and dwellings on either side. The potential, he felt now, was almost limitless.

Frustrated with himself for having already wasted time out by the lake, he made his way down a narrow incline until he reached the bottom, and then he began to walk out into the valley. Wiping sweat from his cold, clammy forehead, he pushed through the growing sense of weakness and tried to ignore a slight sense of breathlessness.

"New Soboltonland," he said loudly, already wondering whether he might be able to salvage some of the old settlement and somehow drag it to the new place. "I like the sound of that."

He turned to look toward the far end of the valley.

"I think -"

Before he could finish, a wave of dizziness passed over him. He tried to stay upright, but for a fraction of a second he couldn't quite distinguish between the ground and the sky, and he quickly fell back and landed with a thud against the hard dirt.

Staring up at the sky, he waited for the dizziness to end. He'd had little spells like this a few times in recent days, and they always passed quickly enough. Now, as he felt his senses returning to their normal state, he sat up and took a deep breath, before looking down once more at his injured right hand.

The wound was much redder and much more swollen than before, and after a moment he reached out and wiped some thick, glistening pus from the edges. He closed and opened his fist, but even this proved much more difficult now since much of the thumb had begun to blacken. Deep down, he knew that something would have to be done about the wound soon, and he worried that eventually he might have to cut the hand off entirely.

He looked at the reddened skin that now stretched past his wrist. If that reached the elbow, he told himself, he'd surely have to act.

"Is this punishment?" he asked himself out loud. "Have I done something wrong?"

Looking up at the bright blue sky, he hoped for some divine message. In that instant, he felt more alone than at any point in his life before, but he quickly reminded himself that he had to remain devoted to his task. Indeed, moments of hardship only made that task *more* important, and he knew that he had to continue to prove himself at every available opportunity.

"I shall do it," he continued, feeling a

growing sense of determination. "I shall move Soboltonland to this spot and build it to great heights. I shall create a temple to the Lord, and all shall hear of it. In this new world, Soboltonland shall become a site of great pilgrimage for all those who have true souls."

Hauling himself up, he once again felt momentarily dizzy, but this time he was just about able to steady himself.

"There is no time for weakness," he continued. "There is only time for strength."

He turned to start the journey back toward the lake, but he froze as he saw three figures standing at the edge of the forest. His heart skipped a beat as he realized that Clara and the two girls had returned, but he realized after a few more seconds that they appeared less ravaged and rotten than before, as if they had begun to return to their former likenesses. Although he couldn't be certain, he began to wonder whether this was some kind of sign that he was now on the right path.

"I'm going to start again!" he called out, waving at them as he began to smile. "Do you see? I'm going to start again and build Soboltonland right here, and you'll see that I was right to bring us here after all! I was listening to the voice of God, and He has brought me here so that I can do His work. I know I made mistakes along the way, and I don't understand why you couldn't come here with me, but what I'm building here will be greater than any one life! People will speak of this place for many years to come! They will visit Soboltonland with glory in their souls!"

He blinked, and in that instant the three figures vanished into thin air.

"Come back!" he shouted, hurrying toward the foot of the slope, then stopping as he saw that they were truly gone. "If you can still hear me," he continued, "know that my heart is pure, and that it swells with the love of thee."

He waited, but all he heard was the silence of the clearing. Somehow, however, he found his answer in this silence, and he told himself that he would let nothing divert him from his task. Soon he set off again, filled with a renewed sense of vigor as he began the long trek back to the lake, focusing on so many grand ideas while trying to ignore the throbbing tight burning sensation in his right hand.

Already, fresh bloodied pus was oozing from the wound.

AMY CROSS

CHAPTER SIXTEEN

Sobolton, USA – Today...

"THIS PLACE GIVES ME the shivers," Mac said as he stopped in the clearing and looked across at the cabin. "I mean, I knew places like this were out here in the forest, everyone did, but I really never wanted to come to one particularly. What did you say we're doing out here, again?"

"We're finding out what's been happening here," John said, stopping next to him as several other officers began to make their way toward the cabin's front steps. "Take it apart if you have to. I don't want any stones left unturned. And if you find any kind of biological material, no matter how insignificant it might seem, I want it bagged and sent off for priority testing."

"What exactly are you hoping to find here?" Mac asked.

"I have absolutely no idea," John told him, "but from what I understand, Lisa Sondnes might well have been held here for all of the past twenty years. I want to know exactly what was going on."

"Twenty years," Mac mused. "That's a long time to be kept as some kind of prisoner."

He paused, before turning to the set of bones in the middle of the clearing.

"And that's not normal either, is it?"

"No, it's not," John told him. "It's a wolf, or rather it used to be."

"Isn't it a little big for a wolf?"

"Absolutely, but I don't think it was just any old wolf." Stepping over to the bones, he looked down at what remained of the skull. Twenty years of exposure to the elements had scrubbed away some of the details, and almost all the flesh – apart from perhaps a few specks here and there – had long since rotted away. "I think this was the leader of the pack. Size matters in these things, doesn't it? I don't know about you, but if I was a wolf, I wouldn't even *think* about challenging another wolf that was this huge. I imagine the debate over who got to lead the pack must have been fairly short. That's if there was even a debate at all."

"I thought there weren't any wolves near Sobolton."

John turned to him.

"That's what everyone says," Mac added with a shrug.

"I know it's what everyone says," John replied, "and to be honest, I'm wondering *why* everyone says it. Is it part of some collective refusal to acknowledge the truth? Or is there something else going on here?"

"I really don't know what you're getting at," Mac said, "but I hate to think that there were wolves in the forest anywhere round these parts." He stared at the bones for a moment longer. "Especially if they're as big as that. A wolf that size could damn near swallow a medium-sized person whole without even chewing.

"I want the bones collected as well," John explained. "Take plenty of photos, and then bag it all up. And check the ground under the bones as well. I don't know what might be there, but I guess it's possible that some organic material could have been preserved." He turned and looked at the cabin, where several officers had already gone inside to start their work. "I want to know exactly what's been going on here during the twenty years Lisa Sondnes was missing."

***

"It's kind of grim," Cassie said, shining her

flashlight down into the narrow space beneath the hatch in the cabin's floor. "She can't have been down in this hole for twenty whole years... can she?"

"There's room to turn around," John pointed out.

"Sure, but..." She paused for a few seconds, as if she couldn't quite comprehend the horror of that kind of captivity. "It's inhuman."

"That might be the correct word to use," John said, "but no, I don't think she was trapped in this space for the entire time she was here. She still had some muscle mass, she seemed to have been able to walk around, otherwise the wastage would have been much greater. So I think perhaps she was either put in here sporadically, or maybe she was only put in when she needed to be punished."

"Punished by who?"

"By Eloise's father," he explained.

"You mean Little Miss Dead? *Her* father?"

"He kept her here," John continued, "and at some point during her captivity, she became pregnant and gave birth."

"Do you think he..." She paused again. "I mean, do you think she..."

"Do I think she wanted that to happen?" he replied. "I don't know. That's another thing that I need to ask her just as soon as she wakes up, but..."

Spotting something down in the cramped

space, he reached out and took Cassie's flashlight. Crouching down, he shone the beam deeper, and he realized that he could make out some scraps of paper.

"Hold this," he said, handing the flashlight back to her before swinging his legs over the side and starting to climb down into the narrow space.

"What did you find?" she asked, as other officers worked nearby.

"Maybe something, maybe nothing," he replied, pulling some roots aside and then lifting up what turned out to be some very old, very tattered paperback books. "Or maybe some paranormal romance novels that look like they were picked up a while back."

"My grandma reads those," Cassie told him.

He looked up at her.

"She can get through one in a single sitting," she continued. "She's eighty-six years old, bless her, and she just loves to read those books, especially when there's some hunky topless dude on the cover."

John looked at the cover and saw that there was, indeed, a photo of a semi-naked woman being held in the arms of a semi-naked male model.

"Taken to the Raven Master's Hall of Love," he read out loud, "by Declan T. Warner."

"I think I might have heard of that author," Cassie suggested. "He's one of Grandma's favorites.

He's written, like, hundreds and hundreds of books and they all seem pretty similar. But what do you think these things are doing down there?"

"I think someone wanted Lisa Sondnes to have reading material," he explained. "That suggests a degree of care." Reaching down, he pulled out a few more books. "Imagine being stuck down here for any length of time. You'd lose your mind. Clearly he didn't want that to happen to her, so he tried to provide her with some comforts. I'm fairly sure I remember that the Lisa of old was a fan of these books, so it's also someone who knew her well."

He looked at another cover.

"*My Love for the Wolf King's Brother*," he whispered, once again reading the title out loud, "by Jessica Molshenberg."

"I can't read those things myself," Cassie said. "They're way too soppy."

"They're very romantic," John observed. "The word 'love' is in most of the titles. Tell me, do these books usually end well for the protagonists?"

"Pretty much always," Cassie explained. "Grandma likes her HEAs."

"HEAs?"

"Happily ever after," she continued. "Don't get me wrong, the characters always go through some really tough stuff, but it makes them stronger and eventually they come out happy at the end.

People like Grandma don't like a sad ending."

"I doubt many people do," John murmured, still sifting through the books. "But that's not how the real world works, is it? Happy endings are few and far between."

"Are you speaking from experience, Sir?"

"I'm sure it's a pretty universal experience," he suggested, before passing the books up to her and starting to climb out from the space beneath the floor. He had to grip one of the larger roots particularly hard before he was able to haul himself over the edge. "But what happens when the fairy-tale ending of these stories collides with the harsh reality of the real world?" Standing up, he took a moment to straighten out the creases in his uniform. "Do you just accept the way things go? Or do you refuse? Do you fight and fight, do you do whatever it takes until you force through the ending that you want? How does that even work? Can you force happiness?"

"I'm not sure," she said cautiously, "but..."

Looking down into the space, she tried to imagine what it must have been like for Lisa to be trapped down there. A shudder went through her bones as she realized that she simply *couldn't* imagine all that horror.

"Are you suggesting," she continued finally, "that he kind of... made her go down there until she was willing to give him the happiness that he thought they both deserved?"

"I think he wasn't able to let go of the dream," John replied darkly, "but there's still one part of the whole mess that doesn't quite make sense to me. In the midst of so much horror and torture and pain, how did the pair of them end up having a child together?"

CHAPTER SEVENTEEN

Soboltonland, The New World – 1701...

"GLORY," HENRY SOBOLTON WHISPERED softly in the darkness, as a fire burned nearby. "Souls... of the righteous. Men will come. All good people... Soboltonland... I..."

With his eyes closed and clammy sweat running down his forehead, Henry turned a little to his right. He tried to open his eyes, but the effort was immense. All evening he'd been feeling strangely hot, and although he'd tried to sleep the sickness off, he felt now as if something was very wrong. His right hand felt so tight that he was sure it might burst, and he knew that a kind of darkness had slowly spread up his arm and was almost at his shoulder.

"Dear Lord," he said, looking out beyond the wooden shelter and seeing the vast starry sky above, "I am your humble servant. I beg of you, give me time to complete my work for you. I have so much love in my heart and I -"

Before he could finish, he heard a scrabbling sound nearby. He turned and looked toward the lake. Telling himself that he was imagining things, he watched the darkness and realized after a few seconds that something was moving a little way from the shelter. He blinked a couple of times, hoping that his family might appear again, but instead a whitish-gray wolf stepped into view, staring back at him intently.

"What are you doing here?" Henry asked, feeling a rush of fear as he realized that he was powerless to defend himself. "What do you want? Get away!"

The wolf showed no response, instead merely continuing to watch him.

"Get away, I tell you!" Henry shouted, somehow finding the strength to sit up slightly. He grabbed a rock from nearby and threw it, hitting the wolf's flank and sending it scampering away. "That's right," he gasped, slumping back down on his back. "You're not welcome here. This is a place of... the Lord."

He stared up at the shelter's rough wooden roof, but a moment later he heard a sniffing sound.

He turned and saw that the wolf was much closer now, almost under the roof, staring down at him with eyes that seemed strangely intelligent.

"Go!" Henry hissed, barely able to find the strength now to speak. "Or do you mean to finish me off? Is that your wish? Then do it! Do the Devil's work and kill me! Eat me alive, if you must, but know that other men will be guided to this spot and they shall finish my work!"

The wolf watched him for a moment longer, before turning and walking out of Henry's field of vision.

"That's right," Henry sneered. "I'm glad you finally got the message. There's no place here for..."

He looked up at the wooden ceiling again.

"For heathen creatures," he continued as his breaths became harsher yet more shallow. "Only the most perfect of souls can enter Soboltonland, souls that have earned that right. My Clara... she would have been perfect here, she..."

His voice trailed off as he imagined Clara, Belle and Mary living with him in this wonderful new place. He knew with all his heart that he would be able to make them happy, and that they could have enjoyed long and peaceful lives if only they hadn't been struck down during the crossing. He still had no idea why they had died while he had lived, and he felt great sorrow in his heart as he realized that they had been deprived of such a wonderful chance.

"It should have been me," he groaned. "They should have lived, and I..."

As he fell silent, he realized that he could hear a strange cracking and splitting sound coming from somewhere nearby. He turned to look at the fire, which had begun to burn out, but the sound seemed to be rising up from further beyond the shelter. The more he listened, the more he realized that there was a sickly crunching element to this sound as well, accompanied by what seemed to be the tearing of meat. As the sound continued, it seemed more and more strange and unnatural, and finally Henry heard a series of slow, agonized grunts.

He had no idea what was happening, but the sweat was pouring down his face now and his eyes quickly slipped shut. As the strange sound continued, Henry Sobolton slipped away into a deep and fevered sleep.

***

When his eyes opened again, he immediately realized that several hours had passed. He was still in the shelter, and the fire was somehow stronger now, and his forehead felt cooler and less clammy.

A moment later, hearing footsteps, he turned to look over at the lake. The footsteps continued, and finally a naked woman stepped into view, although she immediately stopped when she saw that Henry was awake.

"Who are you?" he gasped, barely able to see her eyes behind a shock of thick dark hair that covered part of her face. "What are you doing here?"

The woman instinctively stepped back and looked around, as if she was on the verge of running away.

"Who are you?" Henry asked again. "I demand to know! Where did you come from? Why are you naked? What do you want?"

He waited for an answer, but the woman seemed almost paralyzed by fear. She looked around for a moment longer before turning to him again, and this time the light of the fire managed to catch her large, dark eyes as she glared back at him with great fear.

"I..."

Henry tried to sit up, but he immediately realized that he was too weak. He tried again, before slumping back down and letting out an exhausted sigh. In ordinary circumstances he would have chased the woman away, or captured her and tied her down so that she would have to answer his questions, but in his current state he could do no such thing. Instead he could only stare at the shelter's wooden roof as he heard the woman's footsteps edging closer.

Finally she leaned over him, staring down into his eyes with an expression that hinted at great wildness.

"Who are you?" Henry whispered, blinking a few times before finally his vision blurred for a moment; when it cleared again, he instead saw his beloved dead wife Clara. A smile reached his lips. "Can it be true?" he asked. "Have you found your way back to me?"

He watched as Clara took a piece of fabric and began to wipe his forehead. The fabric felt so soft and cool, and after a few seconds Henry let out a gasp of relief. He knew not how, but he felt certain now that Clara had been returned to him and he could only assume that the Lord had somehow arranged for this mercy. Over the next few minutes, he relaxed for the first time in years as Clara tended to him gently.

"I have longed for you," he said softly. "I have counted the years since I lost you. Thirteen have passed, I believe. I must look so old and rough to you now. I have not seen my own reflection since I arrived in this new world, nor do I wish to do so. I only hope that my face now does not horrify you."

He waited as she continued to clean his skin.

"Why do you not speak?" he asked, tilting his head slightly and looking up at her. "Clara? Say something. I should so dearly like to hear your voice again."

He saw a glimmer of guilt in her eyes as she turned and walked over to fetch something from the other side of the shelter. Somehow he felt so much safer now, and so much more at ease, just knowing that his dear Clara was nearby. He wanted to ask her about the children, to beg her to tell him whether they too had somehow miraculously survived and followed him into the wilderness, but he knew better than to pepper her with questions. For now he was content just to bathe in the warmth and wonder of her presence, and to allow himself to believe – after so much suffering – that finally his quest to find meaning in this strange new world might lead to glory.

As she returned and began to clean the wounds on the other side of his face, Henry closed his eyes. He focused on the rhythm of her breath, and the exquisite beauty of her touch, and he felt almost as if the act of speaking might disturb some special holy union that even now hung in the air between them. In truth, he had never felt truly like himself ever since losing his family, yet now he felt as if his own soul was being poured back into the empty waiting husk of his body. In this way, he was filling up with love and honor and duty and purpose all over again.

And as he drifted off into peaceful sleep, he felt truly blessed, and he realized that he could hear a voice humming a beautiful melody.

CHAPTER EIGHTEEN

Sobolton, USA – Today...

AS HE LOOKED OUT at the scene beyond his office window, Robert Law saw a couple pushing their stroller along the sidewalk. He smiled briefly, but after a moment the smile began to fade as he remembered the terrifying scenes he'd witnessed – hallucinated? - during the night.

Wolves had filled the streets, tearing people apart as the entire town of Sobolton fell into a state of utter disaster. He remembered the agonized scream of a woman who was being ripped to pieces by an angry pack, and he thought of the utter terror he'd felt as he'd realized that nowhere was safe. Although he still couldn't quite be sure *how* he'd seen those things, he was unable to shake a growing sense of dread and a fear that the awful vision hadn't merely been imagined.

What if, instead, it had been a glimpse of the future?

"Mr. Law?"

Startled, he turned and saw that Eloise was looking up at him from her spot on the beanbag in the corner of his office.

"This story's scary," she continued, holding up the copy of *The Haunting on Winchester Road* that she'd taken from John's office. "I don't know if I want to keep reading it."

"That Myers guy's a notorious schlock merchant," he told her. "Not that I've read any of his crap, but I've heard enough about it."

"Mommy reads books that aren't as scary," she added, sounding increasingly uncertain. "I like those better, because I always know that they're going to end with nice things happening to the good people, and all the bad people will be made to go away. But in this one, even though I've only read the first three chapters..." Her voice trailed off as she looked down at the book again. "I'm scared that the bad people are going to win."

"Sometimes they do," he whispered.

She looked up at him again.

"Nothing," he added, stepping around the desk and limping over to the beanbag, then reaching down for the book. "You shouldn't be reading that.

You're too young. Come on, the last thing I want to do is give you nightmares. I'm sure you've got more than enough fuel for some of those already."

She hesitated, and at the last second she pulled the book away.

"No," she said, "I think... I think I want to keep trying. Even though it's scary, I might be able to learn something from it."

"What do you think you'll learn?"

She thought for a moment.

"How to fight bad people," she said finally. "How to *really* fight them. Mommy used to try to hide the truth from me, but you can't always hide, can you? I think sometimes you have to be brave."

"You're a very smart and mature young girl," he told her. "More than a little girl your age has any right to be."

"Sometimes I think I remember things that didn't happen," she continued. "Things that *can't* have happened. Do you ever do that?"

"What kind of things?"

She paused.

"I think I remember... floating," she said cautiously. "I remember waking up and I was floating in really cold water. I looked up and someone was looking back down at me from above the surface, I think... I think it was a wolf. And then, before I had a chance to try to swim back up, the water started to crackle all around me."

"It crackled?"

"I felt it getting harder. It only took a few seconds, it was like the water froze really fast and I tried to reach out but it was already too late. The water froze so fast that I was trapped, and I tried to cry out but I couldn't. I could still see the wolf staring down at me as the ice became hard... hard like a diamond... and then I was frozen and I couldn't get away. The cold got into me, it froze my blood and I could feel myself starting to fall asleep. I didn't know whether I'd ever wake up again. I think I almost didn't."

"You remember being in the lake as it froze," Robert whispered, shocked by her admission. "I don't understand how that's possible."

"I had horrible dreams," she told him. "They hurt so much. It was like someone was slowly taking me apart."

"The autopsy," he continued, as tears began to fill his eyes. "You... felt it, at least partly. I realized that you maybe noticed it, but I had no idea that you felt any pain. Eloise, you have to understand, I never would have done that if I'd known. I was trying to find answers for you. I'm so sorry that I hurt you."

She stared at him, before smiling.

"You're funny," she said finally, before looking back down at the book again. "I like you. I'm going to try to read more of the book, at least another chapter or two. I want to find out if I'm brave enough to keep going."

"Oh, I think you are," he replied. "In fact, I think you might be one of the bravest people I've ever met."

***

"That's horrific," Carolyn said, standing in front of the desk as she tried to make sense of what she'd just heard. "Poor Wendy. I mean... who would do something like that to her?"

"We're looking into it," Toby replied, "but so far it seems like it might have been some kind of random act of violence."

"*Extreme* violence," Sheila added. "There was blood everywhere. One of her eyes -"

"Yes, we get it, Sheila," Toby said firmly, cutting her off. "It's all going to be in the preliminary report if anyone cares to read that."

"I don't mind telling you that we've been absolutely run off our feet all morning," Carolyn continued. "I spoke to Sheriff Tench just now, he's out at the cabin but he's on his way to link up with another team that's searching the river."

"Huh," Toby said, clearly unimpressed.

"I just want a normal day," Carolyn continued. "One normal day. Is that too much to ask?"

"Do you ever think that things were calmer when we had Sheriff Hicks around?" Sheila replied.

"John Tench is a good man," Carolyn said firmly.

"He might be a *great* man," Sheila admitted, "but that doesn't mean he's a great sheriff. He's an outsider, he doesn't know Sobolton. I know that's why he got the job in the first place, people thought that we needed some fresh blood and a new perspective, but at what point do we all acknowledge that the plan just isn't working?"

"He turned up just as Sobolton experienced some really heavy stuff," Carolyn pointed out. "The little girl was found pretty much at the exact moment he started."

"Excuses only last so long," Toby suggested.

"I'm not making excuses," Carolyn replied, struggling to contain a growing sense of frustration. "The guy's been here for a matter of months, that's not long enough for anyone to make a judgment call just yet. You need to cut him some slack and support him, okay? This whole mess is going to tie together eventually, and you'll see that John Tench is ten times the sheriff that Joe Hicks ever was. A hundred times, even!"

"Alright," Toby said with a grin, "I didn't mean to be mean about your boyfriend!"

"Grow up," she replied, making no effort to

hide her obvious disdain for his comment. "I think someone needs to remind you that Sheriff Tench is your boss, and when he tells you to do something, it's not your job to start asking dumb questions. Your job is to follow orders."

"Relax," he chuckled, "there's no need to get so defensive."

He turned and grinned at Sheila.

"Is it me, or is someone getting a little too defensive here?"

Sheila smiled.

"I'm pretty sure," Carolyn said firmly, "that both of you have things to be doing right now. So why don't you get on and do them, or do I have to tell Sheriff Tench that you've been slacking off?"

"Come on," Toby said, heading away along the corridor. "Let's get this paperwork filed. I'd hate for the great Sheriff John Tench to find himself unable to solve all these crimes, just because a few of us stopped to have a chat."

"He's a good man," Carolyn said as she watched the pair of them walking away. "He's going to sort everything out, and soon Sobolton'll be in a much better place. Just wait. You'll see that I'm right."

She paused, but she could hear them still talking and laughing as they disappeared into one of the rooms, and she felt her blood starting to boil.

"I have faith in him," she added. "After all

the years of failure under Joe Hicks, Sobolton's finally going to get sorted out and set straight by John Tench. Because he's a good man."

CHAPTER NINETEEN

Soboltonland, The New World – 1701...

BLINKING IN THE BLINDING light of morning, Henry Sobolton sat up and realized that he felt...

Better.

Healed.

Barely able to believe this change, he looked out from his little shelter and saw the lake's surface glittering calmly under the light of the sun. The scene was so utterly beautiful, so beguiling, that for a moment he felt as if he was in the midst of a whole new sense of calm. Finally, however, he got to his feet and – although he felt a little stiff and sore in places – he stepped out from the shelter and looked around.

"Clara?" he called out.

He waited.

All he heard now was the sound of the lake's water lapping gently at the shore.

"Clara?"

He turned the other way, but he still saw no sign of her. A flicker of fear ignited in his heart, warning him that she might unaccountably have been snatched away from him again, but he quickly drowned that fear in the certain knowledge that no god would ever be so cruel. She had returned, and that meant she was back for good, even if in this particular moment she might have headed off on some errand. He knew full well that she often had trouble sitting still when there were jobs that needed doing.

"Clara?" he shouted again, much louder this time, and he imagined that she couldn't possibly have gone so far away that she wouldn't be able to hear him now. "Where are you? I'm awake and I long to see you again!"

He waited.

Silence.

"I long for your touch," he continued, lowering his voice again, not wanting to scare her by sounding too loud. "I long for your whispers. I long for your company."

He made his way right down to the shore, until the cold water was lapping at his bare feet. As he looked around once more, however, he began to feel an overwhelming sense of loneliness. He knew that Clara couldn't have gone too far, yet somehow he could tell that there was nobody else around for miles. He looked the other way, determined to spot at least the slightest hint of a presence, yet still there was nothing.

When he examined his injured hand, however, he saw clear evidence of her work. The swelling had gone down massively, and the skin had lost almost all its previous redness. The center of the wound, meanwhile, no longer showed any evidence of infection, although the edges were marked by what appeared to be some kind of leaf or spice extract that had been rubbed into the damaged area. He tried to pick the spice out, only to wince and stop as he found that there was still some tenderness. He had no idea exactly what had been done to fix the damage so quickly, but he told himself that Clara was a woman, and that women tended to know much more than men about these things.

"Where are you?" he whispered now, still looking all around and trying to see even the slightest hint of her return. "I *need* you."

***

Hours and hours later, with the sun starting to dip in the sky and the shadows lengthening, Henry tossed another clutch of branches onto the fire he'd been building. The flames rippled and crackled, but Henry's attention was focused on the shoreline as he looked both ways and saw that Clara still wasn't on her way back.

Deep down, he worried that she might be lost out there in the wilderness, so he turned back to the fire and threw on some more branches. These particular branches came from a little further away, but he'd learned over time that they tended to produce darker smoke, and he hoped that this smoke might guide Clara back out from the forest. He couldn't help watching the treeline, convinced that she was going to appear at any moment.

Yet as he continued to tend the fire over the next few hours, and as the sun dipped to bring darkness back to Soboltonland, Henry found himself feeling more and more forlorn.

Adding some more branches, he felt the welcome heat of the flames, but when he turned to look around he realized that now the fire's brightness made it harder for him to make out any details in the surrounding night.

And then, hearing a rustling sound, he turned and looked toward his shelter, and he was just about able to see the shape of a human figure.

"Clara!" he called out, rushing toward her, then stopping as he realized that this was not his wife at all. "Wait! Who are you?"

The naked woman turned and looked at him, and now Henry understood that this was the same woman he'd imagined in the shelter before Clara had taken her place.

"Have you seen my wife?" he asked. "Her name is Clara, and our daughters might be with her too. Please, I mean you no harm."

In an attempt to prove that point, he raised his hands.

"See? I have no weapons, and even if I did, I wouldn't use them. I just... I saw my wife earlier and I know she's around here, and I'm worried that she might have become lost in the forest."

The woman stared back at him, but she looked as if she might bolt away at any moment.

"Please," Henry continued, stepping forward, "I -"

The woman immediately took two steps back.

"No, don't go!" he gasped, stopping and holding his hands out further. "Do you even speak English? My name is Henry Sobolton, I have traveled here across a vast distance. I'm trying to start a settlement, some kind of refuge for travelers who have followed the same path that I myself have taken. I came here alone, or at least I thought I did, but now I'm so confused. I saw my wife, she was right here and she healed me."

He pointed at the wound on his hand.

"See?" he continued, offering as much of a smile as he could muster. "I was ill. Very ill, in fact. I believe I might have been on the verge of death, but then she came to me and she healed me. Now I'm scared, for if she is lost out there, she might fall victim to any manner of dangerous creature. Please, have you seen her at all?"

Again he waited, and this time he had no idea how else he could get through to the strange woman. She looked around, as if she was scared, before finally she turned to him again.

"I speak your tongue," she said, her voice sounding a little deep yet also fragile. "I learned it many years ago, from the old texts."

"Old texts?" he replied. "What old texts?"

"I shouldn't be talking to you."

"Why not?"

"I just felt for you, that's all," she continued, looking around again, almost as if she was terrified that she might be spotted by someone else. "I saw you suffering a few years ago, and I wanted to help you." She turned to him again. "I shouldn't have left those rabbits for you."

"You..."

His voice trailed off as he tried to make sense of what he was hearing.

"You left those for me?"

"Did you think they skinned and cooked themselves?" she asked.

"I thought I must have done it in some state of delirium," he explained.

"I left them for you," she said cautiously. "I could spare them, and I didn't want to see you starve." She hesitated. "After that, I followed you until you came here. I've been observing you, watching your efforts for a while now. Three years, I believe."

"You've been watching me for all this time?"

She nodded.

"Why?"

"I don't know," she admitted. "I suppose I admired the way you worked. You're different. You're the first human I've ever..." She paused again, as if worried that she might have said too much. "I shouldn't come near you," she added. "My people have never gone near humans, not since you first arrived here from across the ice to the west, and certainly not since more of you came from the east. The last time we had contact, a great cataclysm struck us. It's better if we remain separate. Please, build your settlement here, but be careful not to push any deeper into our territory."

She turned to walk away.

"Stay!" Henry called out, panicking at the thought that he might be left alone again.

She stopped and looked back at him.

"Will you stay, at least until my wife

returns?" he asked plaintively, with a hint of desperation in his voice. "Please? I have been so alone here for so long, and I'm desperate for any human company at all. I have food that I can offer you, and water too, and a fire that will keep us both warm. Won't you stay awhile and tell me more about this land?"

CHAPTER TWENTY

Sobolton, USA – Today...

"HE FELL FROM SOMEWHERE up there," John said, shielding his eyes from the sun for a moment as he looked up toward the top of the cliff. "And then..."

He looked down at the rocks, and at the river that was flowing past. Already two officers were wading through the shallows, while a couple more were checking some thick bracken that had gathered over on the other bank.

"He would have landed down here and probably hit those rocks," he continued, before turning to follow the course of the river as it wound its way through the forest, "and then..."

His voice trailed off.

"We have to find him," he added finally. "I *need* to be certain that he's dead."

For a moment he thought back to the sight of Michael stepping back off the edge. The previous night felt as if it had happened in an entirely different lifetime, yet he kept telling himself that he needed to focus on the facts. Sure, Sobolton seemed to be a place that thrived on the strange and unreal, but he remained convinced that he had to stay centered on calm and rational thoughts.

Michael had fallen.

No-one could possibly survive such a fall.

Ergo, his battered and probably very much bloodied corpse had to be somewhere nearby. The only lingering fear, as far as he was concerned, was that Michael's body might have been washed away, never to be found. And that, he knew deep down, would leave a lingering sense of doubt that he would never be able to escape.

"Sir?"

He turned to see Megan, one of the younger trainees who'd recently joined the department, standing nearby.

"Do you want me to follow the river for a little bit?" she asked, sounding hopelessly lost. "I'm not entirely sure where it goes, but I think from here the first stop is Portman's Cross. That's where it divides for a little bit. I'm no expert, but the dividing bit might be a place where a body could...

snag."

"It's worth a shot," John told her.

"I'll just go and... take a look, then," she replied, but she seemed uncertain for a moment before finally stepping past him.

"Take someone with you," John said firmly.

"Oh, I'll only -"

"Take someone with you," he said again, interrupting her this time. "In fact, I don't want anyone wandering off without a partner. And you need to be armed at all times." He turned and looked at the treeline, and although he saw no sign of movement in the shadows, he couldn't help but worry that the entire forest was now teeming with wolves. "Keep an eye out," he added, "and be prepared to shoot at any wildlife that might come your way.."

"Wildlife?" Megan asked.

"Wolves, primarily," he told her.

"I thought there weren't any wolves around here," she replied, before pausing for a moment. "I mean, apart from the ones that killed old Sheriff Hicks."

"We don't know what we're dealing with," John said, "and -"

Before he could finish, he felt a tightening sense of pain in his gut. Wincing, he tried to hide his discomfort, but he already knew that he hadn't been very successful. Megan was staring at him with a puzzled expression, and he knew that he had to distract her quickly.

"Get moving," he said after a moment. "Find someone to go with you, and see if you can locate anything. And stay in touch at all times. The last thing we need right now is for anyone to go walkabout."

***

As soon as he was out of sight behind some nearby rocks, John slid down onto the ground. The pain in his gut had been coming and going all morning, but now it was most definitely more coming than going. He put a hand on his belly and gritted his teeth, but now the pain seemed almost to be rippling and twisting in his belly, threatening to rise up and burst through his ribs from the inside.

Above, the moon could just about be seen hanging in a pale blue sky.

"Come on, pull yourself together," he whispered, trying an old trick that he often used whenever he needed to stay strong. "You've got this, you just need to stay focused."

He waited, hoping against hope that the pain would fade; instead, he felt as if something had begun to scratch at the insides of his belly, almost as if some kind of form was trying to crawl out. He lifted up the front of his shirt and looked at the bare flesh of his chest, and after a moment he realized that his ribs seemed almost to be shifting slightly beneath the skin.

"I'm hallucinating," he continued, leaning back. "This must be some kind of fever."

Looking at his hands, he expected to see that the wound was festering, that perhaps some pus was starting to ooze out; instead he realized that the wound had almost entirely healed, and he realized that he could move his fingers as if they had never been broken at all. He had no idea how, but in the space of less than twenty-four hours his crippled hands had managed to mend themselves.

Sitting up a little, he clenched his teeth as he felt the pain churning once more in his belly. All he knew was that he had to push through, that he didn't have time to get sick; part of him, too, was desperate to prove Doctor Law wrong, to show him that there was no need to stop or rest. As the pain continued to grow, however, John realized that in his current state wouldn't even be able to take charge of the investigation or drive himself back into town. He knew that he had to be strong, that he had to take control, yet in his current weakened condition he wasn't even sure that he could stand up.

And his heart...

His heart was pounding relentlessly in his ears, like the beating of some infernal drum that was about to shatter his skull from the inside.

Reaching into his pocket, he tried to find his cellphone, only to remember that it was gone. He wasn't even sure who he could call, although he supposed that Doctor Law might be able to help. At the same time, he remained convinced that he'd be absolutely fine if he just waited another minute or two. John Tench had never been the kind of man who went to others and asked for assistance, or who tried to share his problems and burdens with other people; instead he'd always worked to deal with matters privately, and the thought of asking for help now made him feel embarrassed, ashamed and like a complete failure.

"You don't have time for this," he said under his breath, as if he truly believed that he could give himself a pep talk. "The whole town of Sobolton is waiting for you to pull yourself together and keep them safe. You didn't come all the way out here just to..."

As the pain twisted tighter and tighter, he leaned forward and let out an agonized grunt. He was on all fours now, and sweat had begun to pour profusely from his brow. He was trying to hold something back; he wasn't sure exactly *what* was threatening to burst out, but he felt as if some dark force was trying to take control of his entire body. Still gasping as the pain intensified, he began to wonder whether this might be the end, and his first thought was that he'd never managed to set things straight with his son.

In his mind's eye, he saw Nick sitting in the station's interrogation room and he wondered how he could ever have failed him so badly.

And then the pain burst through, and John began to whimper as he felt his ribs breaking one-by-one. No longer able to even try to understand what was happening, he rolled onto his back and looked up at the moon's ghost as he waited for the end. Something was forcing its way through the back of his throat and up into his skull now, and his vision had become a blurred mess of flashing lights and twisting, deformed shapes that made no sense at all. His ears, meanwhile, were screaming with a high-pitched whining sound as the pressure became greater and greater, and a moment later he felt his shirt starting to tear open, as if part of his chest had begun to inflate and grow larger.

Certain now that the end was coming, he tilted his head back and tried to cry out. The only sound that left his lips, however, was a muffled groan as finally his eyes began to bulge in their sockets and the skin on his face started to tear straight down the middle.

CHAPTER TWENTY-ONE

Soboltonland, The New World – 1701...

"MY PEOPLE WERE HERE before all the others," the woman said, as she sat warming herself by the fire. Night had fallen now and darkness stretched all around. "Before the humans."

Henry watched her face as firelight danced and flickered across her features. He wasn't used to hearing such strange words coming from the mouth of a woman, but he'd already come to understand that he shouldn't interrupt.

"The first humans came from the west, across the ice," she continued, still staring into the flames. "We drew back to avoid them. My ancestors sensed danger immediately, so they retreated and told themselves that they could still live in peace.

Eventually more humans came, this time from the east. They arrived from across the ocean and tried to set up a new home here. Soon they came into contact with the others from the west, and let's just say that they didn't get on very well. Humans always find reasons to fight other humans, don't they?"

"How long ago was this?" Henry asked.

"Before my time. But the stories have been handed down from generation to generation."

"I've heard about people who were here before us," he replied. "I've heard them called savages, although sometimes I wonder whether that's the wrong way to describe them. Sometimes I think this is their land, and that we have no right to take it."

"Those people exist," she replied, "but they're human, just as you're human." She paused. "My kind are not like them. At least, we weren't, not originally. Not before the final battle."

"What final battle?"

"It happened many hundreds of years ago. The humans from the east eventually abandoned their settlements, but by this point they had come into conflict not only with other humans, but also with my own kind. With the wolves. When the last of them were leaving, a battle took place between one of these humans and one of my ancestors. It's said that a great storm had been brewed up by the gods, and that their faces could be seen in the clouds as the battle unfolded. Finally one of the gods struck the combatants down with a bolt of lightning, ending the battle by merging the two fighters and turning them into one form."

"That sounds... dramatic," Henry pointed out, although he bristled at the idea of these gods. After all, he was certain that only one true god existed. "And unlikely."

"Since that day," she continued, looking over at him, "my people have been cursed by the ability to become like you. We can walk the land in our original forms, or we can change, just as I changed so that I could come and help you. We have learned your language, too."

"How?"

She paused, and now she seemed a little uncomfortable.

"By walking among you," she explained finally. "Your kind haven't noticed, but in the centuries since more of you arrived, a few of us have volunteered to mingle with your settlers and learn their ways. These volunteers then returned and taught us much about you, and we realized – as our ancestors realized – that we should stay far away from you. The problem is, however, that this time you insist on spreading as far as possible across the land. Our leaders fear that soon we shall have nowhere to call our own."

"What about this place?" he asked, looking round at the darkness. "Is *this* your land?"

"Would it matter?"

He turned to her again.

"You'll just take it anyway," she sneered. "You'll probably want it even more if you know that it belongs to others. We've learned that the hard way."

"We can share."

"Share?" she replied, clearly disgusted by that word.

"I just want to build somewhere that's new," he told her. "Somewhere that's free of all the sin and vice of the world I left behind. I have traveled a long way to get here, and it's something of a miracle that I survived this long. I believe that I am here for some divine purpose."

"Indeed," she murmured, looking at the flames again. "You are just like all the others. You're chasing the earlier humans off their lands, and eventually you'll come for us too. When we're in our wolf forms, you consider us to be nothing more than vermin."

"Wolf forms?" He watched her for a moment longer. "I don't understand."

"I know you don't," she said, before pausing for a moment to think. When she looked at him again, her eyes were filled with guilt and fear. "I shall have to show you."

***

A few minutes later, standing a little further from the fire, Henry watched as the woman seemed to be preparing herself for some ordeal. She was naked as she rubbed the sides of her arms, and finally she turned to him again.

"My name is Clanath," she said, and now her voice was trembling with fear. "That's close enough, anyway. This is the last time we shall meet, Henry Sobolton. Perhaps I shouldn't have saved you, but I wanted to help. You seem like a good man, if such a thing exists. I might have been wrong, but..."

Her voice trailed off for a moment.

"I have never let anyone see this before," she added. "I hope it will make you understand how our people can never mix."

He opened his mouth to reply, but he held back as he realized that he still felt so utterly confused. This Clanath woman seemed to speak of some great hidden knowledge, and he couldn't yet decide whether or not she might be completely out of her mind. Part of him wanted to strike her down and punish her for heresy, for speaking of impossible things like angry gods and ancient battles, but he knew that striking her would never work; instead he wanted to talk to her, to make her understand that she was wrong and to teach her about the one true power.

To convert her to his way of seeing the world.

And then, as he was trying to work out how to put such thoughts into words, he saw that Clanath was kneeling on the pebbles, and he watched as she arched her back. A splitting, cracking sound began to break out from her bones, almost as if she was in the process of ripping her own body apart.

"What are you doing?" he asked cautiously, stepping forward. "This cannot be right."

"Stay back," she growled, and now her eyes had begun to bulge from their sockets. "This is the only warning you'll understand. After this, you must leave this place and never -"

Suddenly she let out an anguished grunt and leaned forward, pushing her back up as if her spine was about to bend and snap. On all fours now, she appeared almost to be trying to stretch her torso. Light from the fire still danced across her naked body as her ribs began to split open, but precious little blood was lost as she rolled onto her side and cried out. Henry took another step forward, desperate to help, but in that moment he saw that her face had begun to split down the middle, revealing a darker protuberance that was already forcing its way out. Her body was still spitting and creaking and groaning, and now patches of dark fur were sprouting to cover the shifting, churning muscles and bones beneath.

"This is ungodly," Henry stammered, wondering whether he might be imagining the whole thing. "This should not be allowed."

In that moment Clanath began to rise, but now she was barely human. Still on all fours, she stretched our her arms, but they were arms no longer; instead she had taken on the appearance of some strange animal, and Henry could only watch as she continued to shift until finally he recognized the beast before him. He told himself that he had to be wrong, that he had just witnessed something impossible, but finally Clanath – or the creature that had once been Clanath – turned to him and revealed the eyes of a wolf, before letting out an ear-splitting howl that forced Henry to cover his ears with his hands as he took several more steps back.

"This cannot be!" he gasped, as the wolf's howl finally ended. Lowering his hands, he stared at her with a feeling of true shock spreading through his chest. "I know what you are. There is only one thing in all of creation that could ever do something like this."

He hesitated, before grabbing one of the burning branches from the fire and waving it at the wolf, trying to scare the creature away.

"You're a demon!" he screamed, lunging at the wolf and causing it to scamper away toward the trees. "Get out of here! You're nothing but a foul demon, but you shall not have my soul! You shall be chased out from this place! You shall be chased into the deepest pits of Hell!"

CHAPTER TWENTY-TWO

Sobolton, USA – Today...

LOOKING BACK DOWN AT the report on her desk, Carolyn took a moment to try to memorize the passage she was supposed to type into the computer. She heard the station's front door swinging open, but for a few seconds she focused entirely on the passage before quickly turning to the keyboard and starting to type.

"One moment, please," she said, still desperately trying to remember the text, before letting out a satisfied sigh once she was done. At that moment, she looked up at the person who'd just walked through the door. "Good afternoon, how can I -"

Stopping suddenly, she saw a dashingly

handsome man looking back down at her, although her gaze was immediately drawn to the patch covering one of his eyes. For a moment she could only stare; she knew she was potentially being a little rude, but everything about this man seemed designed to attract attention and she was merely thankful that her jaw hadn't begun to hang open.

"Hey there," the man said finally with a brief, knowing smile. He clearly knew the effect he was having. "I don't want to be a burden, but am I in the right place? Is this the office of the Sobolton sheriff?"

"Yes," she stammered, before trying to pull herself together. "It is. How can I help you?"

"Well, I don't think *you're* the sheriff, are you?" he continued, before taking a moment to glance around. "I mean, I guess you could be, but in my experience sheriffs tend to be grumpy, ugly little men and not..."

He turned to her again.

"Not hot little things such as yourself."

"I'm not the sheriff, no," she replied, shifting in her seat a little, unable to hide the fact that she felt extremely flustered. "I'm afraid Sheriff Tench isn't in the building at the moment."

"Tench, huh?" He nodded sagely. "Yeah, that's the fella's name. I heard it somewhere, although I haven't had the pleasure of getting to meet him yet."

"Can I do anything to you?" she asked, before quickly correcting herself. "I mean, can I do anything *for* you?"

"Well, I guess I don't need the sheriff himself," he continued. "I can probably relay my message to pretty much anyone here. Tell me, are you a smart lady? I'm pretty sure you are, you've got very pretty and very intelligent eyes, but I just want to be sure."

"I do my best," she replied.

"Here's the thing," he said. "I believe an item of lost property has been delivered here, and I'd sure like to retrieve it."

"Lost property?" She paused for a moment. "Well, we don't specifically have a lost property department but -"

"It's a little girl," he continued, holding his hand up about four or five feet from the ground, "sorta yay high. Pretty face, very clever. A little too clever for her own good, sometimes. She might have been here for quite some time, but to be honest with you, I only recently became aware that she'd... thawed out and woken up. Sometimes it can take a little while for a scent to carry, if you know what I mean."

"A girl?" Carolyn replied, convinced that he couldn't actually be serious. She immediately thought of Little Miss Dead, but – again – she knew that couldn't be who he meant. "An... actual girl?"

"Living and breathing, yeah," he said, before biting his bottom lip for a moment as if deep in thought. "I think you know the girl I'm talking about. I can see it in your eyes and, besides, your heart-rate just went up a little. More than it did when I walked through the door, I mean. Please don't be offended, but I can sorta tell that all the blood in your body is getting... redistributed right now."

"I'm not really at liberty to divulge any details on -"

"Oh, I'm sure you're extremely professional," he continued, cutting her off. "You don't want to do anything that's not by the book. I get it." He glanced at the clock on the wall. "How about this for an idea? I'll give you some time to talk to your bosses. With Sheriff Tench gone, I'm sure someone has authority. If not, you can always get old Tench on the blower. Have a little discussion and decide what to do, and then I can take the girl home and no-one has to get hurt. The alternative is that I *still* take her home, just with a lot more fuss. Am I making myself clear?"

Staring at him, Carolyn realized that her mouth was indeed hanging open.

"I'll wait outside while you make your decision," the man said firmly. "How long do you think you'll need? I'm in a bit of a hurry, so why don't I give you... ten minutes? Does that sound fair?"

***

"He wants *what*?"

"I know how crazy it sounds," Carolyn replied, keeping her voice low as she saw Eloise sitting on the beanbag and reading. "I tried to call John, but he didn't answer. I don't know what to do, he's just one guy but he seems... confident."

"Who's in charge here while John's away?" Robert asked.

"With Tommy out of action, I guess... Toby?"

"Not exactly the kind of chap you want in a crisis," Robert muttered. "I guess I could go and speak to our visitor."

He waited for a response, but he could already see the fear in Carolyn's eyes.

"Wait here," he continued, putting a hand on her shoulder, "and I'll go and see what this man's all about, okay? Just keep an eye on Eloise."

Grabbing his cane, he began to step past her.

"Be careful," Carolyn spluttered. "He's hot."

He turned to her.

"He's *really* hot," she continued. "Like, irresistible. I don't know much about science, but I've heard about pheromones and stuff like that. It's almost like he was doing it deliberately. He's so hot,

I couldn't even think straight."

"I think I'll manage," Robert replied, "but thank you for the warning."

Rolling his eyes, he began to make his way along the corridor. He really had no idea what was going on, but he was starting to wonder whether Carolyn was losing her mind. As he reached the reception area, he stopped for a moment to look out the main door, and sure enough he saw a kind of rough-looking guy wearing a patch over one eye, sitting casually on the bench beyond the bottom of the steps.

"Funny lookin' fella," he whispered to himself, before starting to make his way toward the door. "I'm not sure about -"

"Don't let him in."

Startled, Robert turned and saw – to his amazement – that Lisa Sondnes was standing over at the other end of the room.

"Lock the doors," she continued firmly, "bolt the windows and get every weapon you have."

"What the hell are you doing here?" he asked.

"There'll be time for a grand reunion later, Doctor Law," she replied. "Right now my daughter is in danger, and there's no way I'm letting that madman get his hands on her."

"But -"

"That's her uncle," she continued, "and if he

takes her away, I'll never see her again."

"Would you mind explaining to me exactly what's going on?" Robert asked.

"His name is Saint Thomas," she replied. "Goofy name, I know, but apparently their father wanted to pay tribute to something from their past. He's named after a saint who lived about eight hundred years ago. The point is, there's a power struggle between the brothers and clearly Saint Thomas thinks that he can benefit by getting control of Michael's only child. I don't know why Michael isn't here to get her himself, I can only assume that he doesn't know what's going on. Not that I want to see him, but..." She paused. "I don't know, I never really understand all the twists and turns that the brothers go through. The point is, I need to get Eloise well away from this place. Away from Sobolton. Maybe even away from the country."

"Hang on a moment," Robert said, shaking his head, "you're confusing the hell out of me."

"I need a car," she told him. "A *fast* car. One that can outrun a wolf. Also one that can potentially hit a wolf on the road and not break."

"That didn't really help."

"My daughter will not be a pawn in their pathetic squabbles," she said firmly. "They can fight all they want, and I don't care who wins. I don't even care what happens to this town. But Eloise doesn't deserve to get drawn into their madness, and they'll only get their dirty hands on her over my dead body. Once we're clear of Sobolton, I think I can protect her. Their influence is very concentrated in this area, but beyond their territory they're basically nothing. Now, are you going to help me or not?"

Behind her, Toby and a few other officers had begun to appear, drawn by the sound of their voices.

"What's going on here?" Toby asked, looking Lisa up and down. "Is this -"

Suddenly they all heard a tapping sound on the door's glass panel, and they turned to see that Saint Thomas was now standing outside.

"Hey there, Lisa!" he called out, clearly amused by the situation as Robert instinctively reached over and locked the door. "Wow, that's not very friendly, is it? I'm starting to think you want me to do this the hard way."

CHAPTER TWENTY-THREE

Soboltonland, The New World – 1706...

WOODEN CHIMES BUMPED AGAINST one another as a breeze blew across the valley. Hanging from strips of thin knotted bark, the chimes were mixed with grass and other threads that had been haphazardly tied into place.

Nearby, Henry Sobolton remained on his knees, praying at the altar of the makeshift church he'd built in a small, open-doored hut at the center of his new town.

"Lord," he whispered, with his eyes squeezed tight shut, "five years have passed now since I saw that wretched demon. They have been five long and hard years, but I have worked tirelessly to turn this place into a monument to your glory. I only question whether..."

His voice trailed off. Part of him wanted to remain quiet. Worried that giving voice to his doubts might be a weakness, he considered staying silent, but deep down he knew that the Lord would already know what was on his mind. Better, he supposed, to be honest.

"I only question whether the demon was chased out for good," he continued. "I saw such an awful, wretched monstrosity, something that I can still barely believe was real. I am so sorry that I wasn't able to chase it into Hell, but I lost it in the forest that night and..."

Again he fell silent, as he realized that the Lord would already know all of this. Finally he opened his eyes and looked straight ahead at the crude wooden boards and the cross daubed on their front. This so-called 'church' was really nothing of the sort, he had to admit, but it was the best that he'd been able to manage. As for the rest of Soboltonland...

Looking around, he saw the dozen or so structures that he'd labored to erect, although none of them were really any better than crude huts. Unable to even make a door, he'd resorted to setting the huts in a kind of circle so that they would protect one another from most of the elements. As he looked at the meager settlement that so far comprised Soboltonland, he couldn't help but wonder whether his constructions were actually a mockery of the very Lord he'd sought to serve. How had he not done better?

In truth, he already knew the answer to that question. He was getting weaker by the month, and he worried that something was very wrong in his body. He hadn't seen his own reflection for many years, and he was glad of that fact. Even when he went to the lake, he was always careful to avoid looking directly into the water, and he knew that he would rather pluck out his own eyes than see his own face.

A moment later he heard a shuffling sound, and he flinched as he realized that *they* were back.

"I thought you might have left me alone this time," he said softly, in a cracked and dry voice. "What do you want? Haven't you tormented me enough already?"

The shuffling sound continued for a few more seconds before stopping directly behind him. He almost turned to look, but he forced himself to remain on his knees in front of the altar.

"Why must you torment me?" he continued as he heard a faint rattling sound, which he knew could only be coming from their throats. "Are you sent by Satan? If so, you might as well crawl back to him and report that you have failed. I shall not be turned from my task. By my reckoning some twenty years have passed since I left England. I still have time to complete my work."

He waited, and a moment later he felt a cold, clammy hand touch his shoulder from behind. A shudder ran through his body, and after a few more seconds he felt two smaller – but no less dead – hands touching his other shoulder.

"Please leave me in peace," he sobbed, not daring now to turn and see the rotten faces of his family. "Why must you do this? What can you possibly gain from driving me to insanity? Are you doing this purely for your own amusement?"

He swallowed hard, and now he realized that he could hear a series of squelching sounds. Looking down, he saw that a couple of thick maggots were wriggling on the ground, having evidently fallen down there and rolled into view. At the same time, he began to notice a distinctly rotten smell mixed with the stench of dirty seawater.

"I am too strong for you," he said firmly, even as he felt the temptation growing in his chest. "I am too strong. I am too strong. I am too..."

He hesitated, and now the anger began to rise through his body. He gritted his teeth before standing and turning to face the rotten remains of his family.

"I am too strong!" he screamed. "Leave me alone! You're nothing but the Devil's filth! Go back to Hell!"

***

Sobbing frantically, Henry remained on his knees at the edge of the lake, staring out at the rippling water. He'd run away from the clearing and had made his way to the site of the original Soboltonland settlement, and now he was contemplating the possibility that his entire mission had failed.

He thought of the lake's depths, and he was already trying to work out how many rocks he might need to put into his pockets in order to make himself sink. The thought of seeing Clara and the girls again – in such an awful state – was simply too much to contemplate, and he supposed that he should simply finish what remained of his miserable life.

Getting to his feet, with tears still running down his cheeks, he began to pick up some of the larger rocks. He dropped them into his pockets, and soon he felt the extra weight starting to pull him down. Part of him was scared of death, yet at the same time he knew that there was nothing more for him to do in this world. Soboltonland had been a foolish, fitful nightmare that was now going to rot away to nothing in the wilderness. He'd failed everyone he'd tried to help and now there was no further purpose in his life.

Once the rocks were weighing him down, he

began to wade out into the lake. Within seconds the water was up to his waist, then his chest, then his chin and finally -

Suddenly something grabbed him from behind, biting into the back of his neck and hauling him out of the water. Startled, he tried to turn and see the creature, but he lost his balance and the rocks dragged him down. He landed with a spluttering gasp in the shallow water, but already the creature had bitten him on the arm and was pulling him further up the shore. Struggling for air, Henry finally slumped down against the pebbles and looked up to see a wolf staring back down at him.

Not just any wolf, either.

Her.

"What are you doing here?" he gasped, trying to sit up but quickly finding himself weighed down by a combination of the rocks and his own soaked clothing. "Why are you interfering?"

The wolf bared its fangs and let out a long, low growl.

"Get away from me," Henry sneered, pulling free so that he could finally stand up again. "I hoped to never see your devilish face again. If you know what's good for you, you'll get out of here, otherwise I'm liable to find my largest knife and gut you!"

He waited, but the wolf merely continued to

growl at him.

Hurrying back to one of his old shelters, Henry searched for one of the knives, but he quickly realized that he'd left them all at the new settlement in the valley. After checking and finding that there was nothing else he could use as a weapon, he took a couple of steps back before turning to look at the wolf. He wanted to scream at the beast, to tell it that it had no place in this world, but at the last second he saw that it seemed to be in pain. He watched as the creature slumped down, and after a few more seconds he realized that he could hear a loud snapping and cracking sound coming from the animal's body.

As he slowly got his breath back, the minutes passed and the wolf's body gradually began to look more human, with the fur folding inward and the bones rearranging themselves to create a more familiar shape. Although he continued to tell himself that this was a monstrous, hellish vision, Henry couldn't help but watch as the woman known as Clanath finally began to take shape before his very eyes. Finally she reached out with one arm and screamed, as if the very act of changing her form had brought her immense pain, and in the end she was left gasping and naked on the shoreline, barely strong enough even to lift her head.

"You have to leave this place," she gasped as soon as she had enough strength. "Go! Now!"

AMY CROSS

CHAPTER TWENTY-FOUR

Sobolton, USA – Today...

"DOES ANYONE SEE HIM?" Sheila called out, as she peered out through the window in Carolyn's office and saw only an empty parking lot.

"Not on this side," Toby replied, watching through another window. "Do you think he just... gave up? He's only one guy. He probably realized he can't do much against a heavily-armed office like this." He pulled his gun out. "I think it's about time we go and show him that we're not cowards."

"Damn it, John, pick up," one of the other officers muttered, before setting her phone down. "I don't get it. Where is he?"

Standing over on the far side of the reception area, Lisa was silently staring along the corridor. Making his way over to join her, Robert watched the side of her face for a moment before following her gaze, but he saw nothing along the corridor except a bunch of doors, some of them open and some of them closed. A moment later, however, Eloise stepped around the corner, and when she spotted Lisa she immediately let out a gasp and raced forward, slamming into her mother and hugging her tight.

"I knew you'd come back!" she sobbed. "Mommy, I just knew!"

"It's okay," Lisa replied, putting her arms around her daughter and then reaching up to ruffle the hair on the top of her head. "I'm here now. Everything's going to be alright."

"Maybe he *has* gone," Robert suggested. "Maybe he was just full of bluster."

"If you believe that," Lisa replied, turning to him, "then you're a fool. And I know you're not a fool, Doctor Law. After all, a fool wouldn't have risen to such a high position in the medical establishment. You've come a long way since Lakehurst."

"About that -"

"You were just doing your job," she told him. "I understand."

"If I could go back and change it, I would," he continued. "When I found out the full extent of what had been done to you, I was horrified. I never wanted to be part of any insane scheme cooked up by Joe Hicks."

"Speaking of Hicks, I hear he got ripped apart by Saint Thomas and his gang of wolves."

"It wasn't a nice way to go."

"Good," she said firmly. "But Hicks wasn't the only one who sent me to Lakehurst. My own father drove me there and walked me right through the front door."

"I'm sorry, Lisa," Robert continued, "but if -"

Before he could finish, they both heard a single loud bang coming from somewhere at the corridor's other end. They turned to look, but already silence had returned.

"He's inside the building," Lisa said, her voice tense with fear.

"How do you -"

"He's inside the building," she said again, more firmly this time. "You don't happen to have any silver bullets around the place, do you?"

"I don't believe we do."

"What about holy relics?"

"I'm pretty sure we're all out. I could check the evidence locker, but..."

"Then we're going to have to be smarter about this," she continued, her mind racing as she struggled to come up with some kind of plan. She thought for a moment longer, and then she turned to him. "Wait... exactly how long ago did you hurt your leg?"

***

"Okay," she said breathlessly a few minutes later, as she led Eloise into one of the side rooms and turned to her, "I need you to be really brave and just wait in here."

"But Mommy -"

"I can't explain right now," she continued, lifting Eloise up and setting her on the edge of a table, then reaching down and moving some hair from across her face. "You've been brave before. You just have to do it for a little while longer."

"I'm sorry I fell down when I was running away."

"You banged your head, huh?"

"I woke up here," she explained. "I think I woke up once before, when I was in the lake. I was so cold, and I went back to sleep again. Then I was here, and I didn't know what was happening or who any of these people were. I just kept hoping that you were going to come and find me eventually."

"And I did. Just like I promised."

"I made it harder for you, though. I never should have fallen over in the forest."

"No, that's fine," Lisa continued. "I think it worked out for the best. While you were in the ice, they couldn't pick up your scent. That's probably why your aunt put you there in the first place. I'm assuming it was her, at least. She was one of the only ones I ever trusted. Then when you were here, it would have taken time for them to pick up your scent again. When you woke up properly, it would have been impossible for them to miss your presence."

She paused, before dropping down onto her knees.

"Do you remember when I told you I had a plan to get us away from here?"

Eloise thought for a moment, before nodding gently.

"I still do," Lisa added. "This is still all part of the same plan, it's just... taking a little longer."

"Why didn't you run away from the cabin at the same time as me?"

"Sweetheart, I tried," Lisa explained, struggling to hold back the tears that threatened to fill her eyes, "but..."

Her voice trailed off.

"Did Daddy catch you?"

"It's okay. I'm here now."

"Where's Daddy?"

"I don't know."

"He's not going to come here, is he?"

"Not while we're still here," she said firmly. "You know what he and your uncle are like. If your uncle's here, that means your daddy isn't, so that's something." She looked around for a moment, checking the windowless storage room for any vulnerabilities. "I can't wait for the day when we don't have to even think about these idiots and their stupid quarrels. And that day *will* come, even if it takes us a little longer to get there."

"The forest was scary," Eloise continued. "Scarier than I thought it would be. I thought it would be empty, but there were so many things and people out there. There was a woman who saw me, but I managed to get away from her. Even then, I kept thinking that I could see and hear things all around in the darkness. I don't know whether I imagined some of those things, or whether they were real, but I got so scared that I didn't even know which way I was going. I tried to follow your instructions, but I got it all wrong. Mommy, I'm really sorry."

"You don't have to be sorry," Lisa told her.

"I'm scared."

"You don't need to be scared either," she replied, turning to her again and kissing her on the forehead. "I'll keep you safe. Always. I don't care about these wolves and their silly traditions and legacies, but if they threaten you then I'll rip their entire world apart." She paused, realizing that she'd probably said too much, and that she was perhaps scaring her daughter. Finally she reached out and took hold of the end of the girl's nose, giving it a twist and causing her to laugh. "There," she added with a smile. "See? We're going to get out of here and we're going to be fine. I promise."

"I don't think I like towns very much," Eloise replied. "I miss the smell of the forest."

"We'll try to find a nice compromise," Lisa said, "and -"

Before she could finish, the door gently bumped open and she turned to see Robert Law.

"We need you," he said cautiously, as a loud banging sound was briefly heard in the distance. "I'm sorry, Lisa, but if we're going to do this, now's the time."

"I'm coming," she replied, getting to her feet and stepping over to the doorway. Once she was out of the room, she turned to Eloise again. "Wait in here," she continued, "and don't come out for anyone except me." She paused. "Or Doctor Law. Do you understand?"

Eloise thought about that instruction for a moment, before finally nodding. She still felt a tightening sense of fear, however, as the door bumped shut and she was left sitting alone. Part of her wanted to hide under the table, while part of her hated the idea of simply waiting around. The more she looked at the door, the more she felt as if she should go out there and try to help, but she knew she should be good and that she really ought to follow her mother's instructions to the letter. The urge to go and see what was happening, however, seemed almost to be bursting out of her, and a moment later she heard voices as several people hurried past the room.

Finally, slowly, Eloise stepped off the table and began to approach the door.

CHAPTER TWENTY-FIVE

Soboltonland, The New World – 1706...

"THEY'VE BEEN WATCHING YOU for years," Clanath explained as she sat next to a fire on the lake's shore, warming her hands. "Keeping an eye on you, I suppose, might be a better way of describing it. At first they saw you as more of a curiosity, but now..."

Her voice trailed off for a moment as she looked all around, as if she expected trouble to arrive from any direction.

"I don't need help," Henry said through gritted teeth. "I can take care of myself."

"You were about to *drown* yourself," she pointed out.

"That was because of the visions," he explained, before shaking his head. "I keep seeing my wife and my daughters. I know they blame me for what happened to them. They've been dead for so long, but they're still haunting me. You have no idea what it's like to see them in this way."

"It's this place," she told him.

"How can that be true?"

"Some places are more prone to such occurrences than others," she told him. "There are... fields of energy, but they're not spread out evenly across the world. I don't think humans are even aware of them. Some might be, but only on a very low level. They feel their impact, but they don't understand why. But my people are keenly aware of this energy, we're able to move through and around it at will. It's concentrated around this valley, among other places, which is one of the reasons why my ancestors chose to make their home here so long ago. I'm sure it's also one of the reasons why you see your dead family."

"Does that mean it's not really them?" he asked. "Is it all in my head?"

"I don't know," she admitted. "The energy certainly could drive you mad and conjure up all sorts of fears from the depths of your mind. Or it could make the spirits more likely to visit you.

Without seeing them myself, I simply cannot say whether what you see is real or not." She paused again. "But you'll find out soon enough, Henry Sobolton, because you have to leave this place tonight."

"Why?"

"The others in my pack aren't happy with you," she continued. "They fear that your settlement might attract more humans."

"I'm the only one here."

"But what if others arrive?" she asked. "The last thing they want is to have a human settlement, perhaps even a town, in the middle of our most sacred land. At first they assumed that you'd simply fail, that you'd die in the mud. Believe me, they're not happy with me for assisting you. Had I not tended to your wounds a few years ago, you'd be nothing more than bones by now and there would be no threat to us."

"Yet you saved me again today."

"I do not like to see a good man die," she admitted. "My people believe that humans can never be truly good. They see you all as a mere irritant. I used to assume that they were correct, but after watching you for a while I began to see goodness in your deeds. And there's something else. When we look into the future, time bleeds and we sometimes pick up traces of what will be. My elders have done this, and they have reason to fear that your Soboltonland will one day thrive."

"Now I'm *certain* that they're insane," he replied grimly. "Look around. There's nothing here, at least not really. Soboltonland is a total failure. I'm a failure too."

"Sometimes the greatest successes are born from failures," she said darkly, before suddenly turning and looking toward the trees. "Time's running out. They're coming. Henry, you need to leave now."

***

"I'm am no fool," Henry said as he stormed through the forest. "You come to me and speak this nonsense, and you expect me to believe that any of it can be true."

"Henry -"

"What is it precisely," he continued, making his way between the trees and down toward the depths of the valley, "that I did, that made you believe I am such a fool?"

"Henry, why won't you listen to me?" she continued, hurrying after him. "They're here right now and they won't leave until they're satisfied. Do you have any idea how much of a risk I'm taking by coming to you like this? They won't be happy that I've warned you, but I'm sure I'll be forgiven if they see that you're leaving."

"I would rather die here."

"I had no idea that you were so stubborn."

"I am thousands of miles from my home," he replied breathlessly. "My wife is dead. My children are dead. I have spent countless years here now, trying to build something in this harsh new land, trying to create a place for all those who truly worship the Lord. I admit that I have had moments of weakness, and I am not proud of those moments, but all this talk of wolves and kingdoms just makes me renew my determination to complete this work."

"Henry -"

"I did not ask for your advice!" he shouted angrily, stopping and turning to her. "For the love of -"

In that moment, he saw that his dead wife and children were standing directly behind Clanath, staring back at him with the same accusing glares that he'd seen so many times already.

"Why will you not let me help you?" Clanath asked, clearly unaware of the ghostly figures that had joined them now in the forest. "This land is vast. I can even help you find a new path. I will travel with you, at least for a while, and we can locate some other place for your venture."

She waited for a reply, but Henry could only stare in horror at the faces of his dead family.

"What's wrong?" Clanath said, looking over her shoulder for a moment before turning to him again. "Henry? What do you see?"

"Are they really there?" he stammered.

"Do you mean..." She paused, before stepping forward. "Do you see your wife again? And your daughters?"

Barely hearing her words, Henry watched as wriggling maggots crawled through Clara's face. He looked at Belle and saw that more than half her head had been eaten away, and that some kind of tentacled creature had made a home in what remained of her skull. Of Mary, meanwhile, there was even less left; the poor girl had wasted away almost to mere bones, and was held together by the smallest scraps of flesh.

"Why did you leave us?" Clara gasped. "Why did you lead us to our deaths?"

"I was trying to save us all," he replied as tears filled his eyes.

"We could have gone home," Clara pointed out. "We would still be alive."

"If I could swap places with you, I would,"

he exclaimed.

"But you cannot," Clara said darkly, "and we have spent so long in the depths of the ocean. Do you have any idea, Henry, how cold and dark it is down there? No sunlight penetrates that wretched chasm. We can see nothing."

"But we feel them," Belle added. "The creatures that live down there. We feel their spindly legs as they crawl over our bodies and burrow into what remains of our flesh. Or we *did* feel them, when we had any flesh to devour. Now we are little more than mere bones, and the sea creatures and the sediment drift between our bare ribs. Sometimes we hear the strangest of echoes. There are things that live down there in the depths, Father. There are huge creatures, monstrosities that no man has ever seen or ever will see. They are ungodly, and you have left us with them."

"I didn't know," he whispered as tears ran down his face. "I swear..."

"Belle is wrong about one thing, perhaps," Clara told him. "She says the beasts in the depths of the ocean are ungodly, but I fear that is not how they perceive themselves. I hear their mighty roars sometimes when they emerge from their trenches. They believe themselves to be gods, and I for one am not sure that I could mount an argument against them. Perhaps they are. And for so long as they remain hidden down there away from all light, let us hope that those of us on the surface never have to find out."

"Clara, please..."

"Henry?"

Startled, he turned to see that Clanath was watching him with an expression of growing concern.

"Who are you talking to?" she asked.

"Do you not see them?"

She turned and looked directly toward the three rotten figures, and then she turned back to him.

"We are the only ones here," she said cautiously. "Why? Do you see your family now?"

Henry blinked, and in that moment the three figures were gone.

"No," he said after a few seconds, as he realized that they had just been figments of his imagination all alone. "No, I do not."

CHAPTER TWENTY-SIX

Sobolton, USA – Today...

THE STRIP LIGHTS FLICKERED slightly as Lisa stepped forward, reaching the turn in the corridor. As soon as she looked around the corner, she saw that Saint Thomas was busy looking through the contents of a filing cabinet in John's office.

"Find anything interesting?" she asked.

"That Wentworth Stone guy was a tad crazy, huh?" he mused, not looking over at her as he continued to leaf through some pages. "I mean, I know my people can get up to some weird stuff, but this nonsense about the swans is truly something else. Quality nonsense, though, so I'll give him that."

He set the file back into its place and closed

the drawer, and then he turned to her.

"Hey, Lisa," he continued, "it's been a while. So you finally managed to get away from my psycho brother. To be honest, I don't blame you. He's a really mixed-up kid. I blame his upbringing."

"You're not taking Eloise."

"Lisa -"

"I won't let you."

"And how are you going to stop me?" he asked, stepping out of the room and then stopping once he was in the corridor. "Let me guess. You're gonna use some kind of 'girl power' to stand in my way. You think confidence and sass can hold me back."

"She's my daughter and -"

"Oh, so you're going for the whole mother bear approach," he continued, sauntering forward. "I've heard people invoke that kind of stuff before. They claim that parents – mothers in particular – can summon up feats of unimaginable strength when their children are in danger. I have no idea whether that's true, Lisa, but there's certainly a limit." He stopped just a few feet from her and shoved his hands into his pocket. "It's a commendable idea, but in this case it just isn't going to work."

"You'll have to get through me if you want to get to her," she sneered.

"I was there that night, you know," he

replied. "The night little Eloise was conceived." He paused, watching the flicker of horror in her eyes. "I heard your screams. I always knew Michael was troubled and... problematic, but I never thought he'd do something like that. I guess he was so determined to make things work out with you, and eventually he stored up all his energy until it came burst out in that unfortunate late-night incident. I thought about coming into the cabin and dragging him off you, but there was part of me that still wondered whether deep down... you were actually enjoying it."

"Go to Hell."

"I need the girl," he continued. "Now that Michael's dead, there's the thorny issue of who should become our new king."

"You don't allow queens, though," she replied. "You'd never want to crown Eloise."

"No, but it's good to get rid of any potential... issues," he said cautiously. "You never know when some idiot might decide to argue for change, so it'd be a good idea for me to carefully sideline any loose ends. Both my brothers are gone now, so I'm pretty much the only possible choice to become the new king. I just really need to tidy Eloise out of the way."

"Then let me take her," she said firmly. "We'll go far from here, we'll go to Europe or even further, and you'll never have to think about her ever again. You and the others can do whatever you want, I really don't give a damn, and we'll never darken this place again."

"You know it never works out that way," he pointed out. "Fate has a way of bringing things round in a kinda circular fashion."

"I'll make sure that doesn't happen," she said as a tear reached her left eye.

"You didn't know he was dead, did you?" Saint Thomas replied. "When I mentioned it just now, you acted like it wasn't news, but now I can see that you had no idea."

"I *hoped* he was dead," she told him. "I'm glad. I just hope it hurt."

"You don't mean that," he suggested. "That's the problem with you, Lisa. Despite everything my brother ever did to you, there's part of you that still clings to that notion of a 'happy ever after' ending. You thought your perfect love story could somehow get back onto the right track. Well, let me tell you, Michael died last night. I don't know the exact circumstances, but we have a way of keeping tabs of these things." He took a step forward, until he was towering over her. "I felt the moment his soul was extinguished," he continued, "and I'm pretty sure that, yes, it hurt very briefly at the end. Not that he probably cared, of course, because by that point he was completely out of his mind."

"Why keep the patch over your eye?" she

asked.

"You're trying to distract me."

"You could grow a new eye when you shift your shape," she pointed out. "Why keep that hideous injury?"

"It's a reminder of a mistake I once made," he replied, briefly lifting the patch so that she could see the damage beneath, "when I got too close to an injured human. I like to think of it as a red badge of courage. I won't ever make the same mistake again."

"What if -"

Suddenly he grabbed her by the throat, swinging her around before slamming her into the opposite wall with such force that she let out a gasp of pain.

"Enough talk!" he snarled, leaning so close to her face that she felt spittle flying from his mouth. "I'm taking Eloise back to the forest, back to the kingdom, and you will never see her again! Get used to that fact, and just forget that she ever existed. She'll be fine, she'll get to live with her own kind. See, that's the problem with your little plan to take her to safety, Lisa. You're forgetting that she's only half human."

He tilted his head slightly.

"Her other half," he added, "is wolf."

"She'll never find out about that!" she hissed. "Let go of me, or I swear you'll pay!"

"Oh, right," he continued, "I forgot. Your plan. What was it, again? Sass? Mamma Bear? Amazonian warrior? Girl power?"

"None of those," she replied, as she struggled to pull free from his grip. "Actually, I was thinking of a wooden cane with a hastily-sharpened silver tip."

Saint Thomas opened his mouth to reply, but at the very last second he heard the faintest hint of a door opening somewhere nearby.

In that moment, Robert Law lunged out from his hiding place in one of the offices and pushed the cane's sharpened silver tip straight into the man's back, twisting it so hard that it cracked against the spine and then burst out through the front of the belly.

Screaming in agony, Saint Thomas spun around with the cane still running through his torso. He grabbed Robert and tried to snap his neck, but at the last second he had to pull back as the flesh around the cane began to burn. Lisa and Robert stepped away in shock as Saint Thomas reached down and grabbed the cane; he was trying to pull it out, but as soon as the silver tip touched his skin he cried out once more.

"Now what?" Robert asked.

"Silver kills them," Lisa told him breathlessly. "Don't ask me how, but it's absolutely lethal to them."

"So what's he gonna do? Just dissolve?"

"That'd be ideal," she suggested.

"Bitch!" Saint Thomas shouted, still gripping the cane. As he turned to her, blood began to run from his eyes and he was forced to double over in pain. He stepped back and bumped against the wall. His hands were shaking violently now as he once again tried to rip the cane out, but every attempt simply brought him more and more agony.

"I don't particularly want to watch a man die," Robert said, turning away. "I've seen enough suffering over the years."

"I *have* to watch," Lisa told him, keeping her eyes fixed on Saint Thomas as he slumped down against the floor. "It's the only way to be sure. I have to know that Eloise is safe."

"You think she'll ever be safe?" Saint Thomas snarled, clearly starting to weaken. "You think I'm the only one who's gonna come for her? Even if I was, you're forgetting that you can never take her away from her true people. She'll always be carrying a wolf inside her. What are you gonna do? Never let her see the moon? Never..."

His voice trailed off for a moment. He let out a faint gasp, and then he slid over to one side, falling down helplessly against the floor.

"Is he... dead?" Robert asked after a few seconds.

Lisa walked over to him. She peered at the

body, before giving it a gentle kick. The dead man's bloodied eyes simply stared lifelessly at the opposite wall.

"He was right, though," she said, turning to Robert. "There *will* be others coming for Eloise. And I know getting her away from Sobolton won't get her away from the wolf she'll always carry in her heart, but... I have to try."

CHAPTER TWENTY-SEVEN

Soboltonland, The New World – 1706...

"WHAT ARE YOU DOING, Henry?" Clanath asked as she watched him using a crude homemade hammer to force two pieces of wood deeper into the muddy ground. "This is not the time to build anything. You have to leave."

"I would rather die here than draw breath in any other place," he told her.

Glancing around across the valley, Clanath saw no sign of movement. She knew the other wolves were out there, however, and she also knew that soon they would arrive in great numbers.

"How can I better make you understand?" she continued, turning back to him. "There is no point building anything. They'll only tear it down when they arrive." She spotted a piece of wood with the name Soboltonland crudely carved into one side, and for a moment she felt a great sense of sorrow for Henry's pitiful attempts to create a settlement. "You're wasting your time. You could do so much, you could really make a difference, just... not here."

"Yet here is where I choose to make my home."

"Henry -"

"If the job was easy," he continued, as he adjusted one of the pieces of wood, "then it would scarcely be worth doing." He set back to work hammering, before adjusting the wood yet again, as if he still wasn't quite happy. "Then again, I wouldn't expect you to understand."

"Because I'm not human?"

He adjusted the wood for a third time.

"Because you're not -"

Before he could finish, he brought the hammer crashing down again, this time hitting his own hand. Letting out a gasp of pain, he threw the hammer aside and pulled back, and he immediately saw that he'd broken several of his fingers.

"Let me see," Clanath said, hurrying over to him.

"I'm fine!"

"You are most certainly not fine," she continued, grabbing his hand and looking at the damage. "You have broken the bones in three fingers."

"How can you be so sure?"

"I heard each of them crunch in turn," she replied, looking into his eyes. "Does it surprise you to learn that my hearing is a little better than yours? As is my sense of smell. In fact, I'm starting to realize that many of my senses are far more heightened than anything you possess."

"Well," he said darkly, "then you're just perfect, aren't you?"

They stared at one another in silence for a moment, from just inches away, as Clanath continued to hold Henry's injured hand. They both seemed to be on the verge of saying something, yet neither of them seemed quite prepared to break the tension that was growing between them, until finally Clanath let go of his hand and turned away.

"I should never have come here," she whispered, as if shocked by something. "I have made the most dreadful mistake."

"In that, we are at least agreed," Henry replied. "I am just a man trying to make his way in the wilderness. I never asked for an audience. I never asked for interference. I used to think that I was waiting for others to arrive, so that they could help me, but now I realize that all along I was merely deluding myself. I understand now that, after my family died, I came out here to lose myself in a new world. Soboltonland will surely die with me, whenever that day might come, but mark my words... I do not need saving."

"Good," she said, letting go of his hands and taking a step back. "That is just as well, for I believe that nobody could ever save you. I can only leave you to your fate, Henry, and I cannot bear to witness what happens next. Only know that I... I tried to do the right thing." She had tears in her eyes now, but after a moment she turned and began to walk away. "I only hope," she added under her breath, "that they will make your death quick."

***

A few hours later, with the afternoon light starting to fade, Henry hauled up another log and propped it against the makeshift wall he'd begun to make. His arms were aching and his injured hand was throbbing with pain, but he told himself that he had to keep working for as long as possible.

Indeed, he supposed that he had to keep working until his last breath.

Stepping back for a moment, he admired his work. Soboltonland was still nothing more than a pitiful collection of poorly built huts and shelters, but at least the place was starting to take shape. He had the grandest of plans in his mind, he envisioned an entire town or even a city, although deep down he knew now that such plans were never going to come to fruition.

Not in his own lifetime, at least.

He headed over to patch of grass that he'd been using to keep his tools safe. Crouching down, he reached for another of the homemade hammers, but then – as he got to his feet – he suddenly began to feel strangely dizzy. He paused, convinced that the sensation would soon pass, yet instead the dizziness grew and grew until he felt as if he might fall at any moment. He put a hand to the side of his head and turned around, and in that moment he began to hear the most horrendous cacophony of noise filling the air all around.

Looking across the valley, his vision starting to blur, he was shocked to see a vast array of movement. He blinked a couple of times, and now his vision cleared to reveal strange buildings that he knew couldn't possibly exist. Some of these buildings were quite tall, while others were squat and long, and they were all made of materials that made no sense in Henry's mind. He turned to look the other way, just as a large carriage rolled by without the benefit of horses.

In a matter of seconds, a world had sprung up that Henry couldn't comprehend at all.

He turned to look the other way, and he spotted a bright sign over a nearby doorway. Squinting, he tried to read the words. He'd never been a particularly strong reader, but after a few seconds he was able to make out the name of what appeared to be some kind of local hostelry.

"McGinty's," he whispered, and then he looked the other way and saw a sign outside one of the buildings on the other side of the road. "Sobolton Sheriff's Department."

Still feeling strangely dizzy, he took a couple of steps forward before stopping again. He allowed the noise and brightness and sheer madness of this strange place to buzz in the air all around, until he felt as if he might scream. Telling himself that he must be having some strange vision of Hell, he felt an urge to cry out, but he managed to stay calm even as the world began to swirl all around him. Fearing that death had arrived, he dropped to his knees and waited for the end. He hung his head in shame, but in that moment the air seemed to drain of all its energy. When he looked up again, Henry found that the strange mad world of his vision was gone, and that now only the bare valley remained with its hodgepodge of scattered shacks that he himself had built.

Sweat was pouring down his face.

"What was that place?" he stammered, barely able to remember the shocking sights that had briefly filled his eyes. "What hellish nightmare did I -"

Before he could finish, he spotted movement out of the corner of his eye. He turned and looked to his left, and to his horror he saw half a dozen wolves slowly making their way from the treeline, venturing cautiously into the valley.

"What do you want?" he said through gritted teeth. "Have you merely come to watch a man die? Or are you here to hurry me on my way?"

He watched as the wolves reached the bottom of the gentle muddy slope. They seemed to be in no hurry, and soon they started walking in different directions. Realizing that they meant to surround him, Henry got to his feet and grabbed another of his crude tools; he knew he could never hope to fight off so many creatures, but he told himself that he could at least give a good reckoning of himself. Yet as the wolves continued with their slow progress, he realized that death at the hands – or jaws – of the wolves would be extremely painful.

"Good," he said under his breath, supposing that pain might cleanse his earthly soul of at least some of its sins. "This is nothing less than I deserve. I shall accept my fate, but in the process I shall also most certainly make some noise." Holding one weapon in his good hand and one in the hand crippled by the hammer, he prepared to make his final stand. "Now," he added, looking at each of the wolves in turn as they stalked ever closer, "which of you shall make the first move?"

He waited, but once again they seemed to be in no rush.

"Come at me!" he screamed finally. "Come and take my life if you dare!"

CHAPTER TWENTY-EIGHT

Sobolton, USA – Today...

TURNING THE HANDLE EVER-SO-CAREFULLY, Eloise pulled the door open and looked out into the corridor. She knew she was being naughty, but she also knew that she couldn't simply wait around in a windowless room forever.

"Lisa, are you sure about this?" a voice called out in the distance as footsteps suddenly began to approach. "Stop and think for a moment!"

Realizing that she was about to get caught, Eloise gasped and pulled back. She shut the door and hurried back across the room, quickly jumping onto the table just as the door opened again and her mother appeared.

"Good girl," Lisa said, grabbing her hand

and pulling her out into the corridor. "Well done for staying put. Now we're getting out of this town, and we're never coming back."

***

Hurrying down the steps at the front of the police station, still holding Eloise's hand, Lisa was already looking around for a vehicle she could use.

"Do you have a car?" she asked Robert.

"Take it," he replied, pulling his keys from his pocket and handing them to her, "but where are you going to go?"

"I have absolutely no idea," she admitted. "I don't have a passport right now, so leaving the country isn't an option after all. I can take her south, though, far away from anywhere these wolves can get to her. Then I can start to figure something else out. We'll need money, I don't know how I'm going to sort that out, but the first priority has to be to get us away from Sobolton." She paused for a moment. "Thank you, Doctor Law. You've helped us so much."

"It's the least I could do," he told her. "Now go. My car's that red one over there. Be careful with her, though. She's a beauty."

Gripping Eloise's hand tighter, Lisa led her toward the car. Glancing around, she couldn't help but worry that fresh danger might appear at any moment and from any direction. She felt desperately weak and she knew she needed to rest, but as she reached the car she told herself that she had to get Eloise to safety. She tried to find the right key, only to drop the entire set. Crouching down, she picked them up again before glancing back toward Robert.

She opened her mouth to thank him again, but in that moment she spotted a familiar – but impossible – figure storming through the station's reception area and heading toward the front door.

"Get down," she stammered, before standing and watching with horror as Saint Thomas pushed the door open. "Doctor Law, get -"

Before she could finish, Saint Thomas ripped the door off its hinges and twisted it around, before throwing it down the steps. Startled, Robert tried to get out of the way in time, only for the door to smash into his legs and knock him over like a cheap skittle.

Lisa froze for a moment, watching as Saint Thomas finished ripping the remains of the cane from his own belly, and then she grabbed Eloise and tried to push her away.

"Run!" she yelled. "Find somewhere to hide! I'll come and find you later!"

"Mommy, I'm scared," Eloise whimpered.

"I know," Lisa replied, turning to see that Saint Thomas had almost reached them. The fury on his face was impossible to miss. "I just need a moment to -"

Suddenly a large wolf lunged into view, jumping over the car and slamming into Saint Thomas. Letting out a shocked gasp as he fell to the ground, Saint Thomas immediately tried to throw the wolf aside, but the creature quickly proved to be far too strong. Pushing him down instead, the wolf snarled loudly as saliva dribbled from its jaws, and so far it seemed able to resist every attempt Saint Thomas made to push it aside.

"Come on!" Robert hissed, limping around them and hurrying to the car. Grabbing the keys, he opened the door. "You're in no fit state to drive, Lisa. Get in the back!"

Trying not to panic, Lisa pulled the other door open. She bundled Eloise into the car and then jumped in, barely managing to pull the door shut before Robert started the engine and hit the gas pedal. The car lurched forward, just as Saint Thomas finally managed to throw the wolf to one side and get to his feet.

"He's coming after us!" Eloise shouted, watching as Saint Thomas began to run after the car.

"I had this little beauty tuned up just last summer," Robert said through gritted teeth, as he raced the car around the parking lot and out onto the street, almost colliding with a low-loader in the process before driving away toward the far end of town. "There's not a lot she can't outrun, not when she's got the open road ahead of her. Stay calm, Lisa. I'm getting you both the hell away from here!"

***

Reaching the edge of the parking lot, Saint Thomas finally stopped as he saw Robert's car disappearing into the distance. Out of breath and still bleeding from the wound in his belly, he paused for a moment before hearing a growling sound nearby. He turned slowly to see that the large gray wolf was slowly stalking toward him, clearly preparing to pounce.

"Now who are you when you're at home?" Saint Thomas sneered, looking into its dark eyes but finding no trace of recognition. "Call me complacent, but I always thought I knew everybody who was everybody round these parts. But you're new in town, aren't you?"

As if to answer that question, the gray wolf snarled again.

"Easy," Saint Thomas continued, holding his hands up in mock surrender. "We're on the same side. At least, we sure *should* be. What got into you, helping those humans like that? Don't you know who I am?"

Glancing around, he saw that startled onlookers had begun to make their way over, shocked by everything that had happened recently in the parking lot. Turning his attention to the wolf again, he narrowed his gaze a little as he tried to work out exactly where this interloper had come from and why he was getting involved in Sobolton business.

"But you're not from any local pack, are you?" he continued, watching carefully for any sign that the beast might be about to strike. "You must know the territory, though. No wolf would just come marching into another pack's homeland and start throwing its weight around. That would just be... rude!"

The wolf snarled yet again.

"And now you're trying to warn me off," Saint Thomas mused. "In my own backyard, you're acting like *I'm* the one who's doing something wrong. Now, I've got to admit, I don't like this turn of events one little bit." Reaching down, he felt some more blood seeping from the wound in his belly. "You're lucky, though," he added. "You caught me when I'm not quite at my best, otherwise by now I'd be measuring your pelt up for my fireplace. I hope you realize that if we're unlucky enough to meet again, I'll be much more inclined to rip your goddamn head off. Think about that before -."

In that moment a shot rang out, and Saint Thomas turned to see two deputies emerging from the front of the station. One of them was carrying a rifle, which he quickly fired into the air again. The wolf turned and watched for a moment, then looked around at the gathering crowd for a few more seconds before turning and racing away across the parking lot.

"Get out of here!" Toby yelled, firing for a third time into the air as the wolf disappeared into the distance, clearly heading back toward the forest. "Goddamn dumb animal!"

"Was that a wolf?" Brenda Pottage stammered, as she and some friends stopped at the edge of the sidewalk. "Was that an actual wolf, right here in Sobolton? I thought there were no wolves around here. That's what everyone has always said."

"Looks like everyone has been wrong," Saint Thomas murmured with a smile, before turning to her. "Perhaps it was more a case of wishful thinking."

"Are you okay?" she asked. "That horrible thing was right in front of you. For a moment I thought it was going to eat you whole!"

"I can take care of myself, M'am," he replied, adjusting his jacket for a moment.

"You're bleeding," she continued, looking at his belly. "Do you need a ride to the hospital?"

"Thank you for your concern, but I'll be absolutely fine." He offered her a smile before turning and starting to walk away along the main street. With each step, his expression became darker as he began to contemplate his next move. "And now, if you'll excuse me, I've got some rather important family business that requires my immediate attention."

CHAPTER TWENTY-NINE

Soboltonland, The New World – 1706...

TREES RUSTLED AS A gentle breeze blew through the forest. For a moment all was still and all was silent, as if the entire land remained untouched, but finally the peace was shattered by a sudden gasping sound.

Hauling himself up, with blood running from several cuts on his face, Henry Sobolton winced as he felt flashes of pain running up his side. He'd managed to drag himself away from the clearing and past the treeline, desperately trying to find somewhere he could hide. A flap of skin was hanging down from his left cheek, revealing the blooded bone beneath, and one of his eyeballs had been pierced by a shard of wood; the pupil was blackened and destroyed, and clear liquid was dribbling from the soft orb and running down to mix with the blood caked around his chin.

A moment later he heard them.

Crawling forward, he told himself that he could still fight. When the first wolf had attacked, he'd been able to hold it off, at least until the others had gradually joined in. Soon, however, he'd found himself surrounded, and the wolves had seemed to take it in turns to snap at his limbs. He'd put up a good defense, but now he understood that no man could fight off such a pack and he knew his only hope was to run. And if running was impossible, then he was going to have to crawl on his hands and knees, while hoping and praying for a miracle.

He could hear the wolves now, however.

He could hear them snarling as they edged closer.

Turning, he flinched as he saw them watching him from their vantage point beyond the trees. The beasts were already spreading out, preparing for another attack, and this time Henry no longer had the crude tools that had helped him earlier. This time he only had his hands, one of which was already wrecked due to his own mistake; he knew that the wolves were liable to rip him apart limb from limb, but he told himself that at least there would be pain, that at least he wasn't going to die alone and shivering on a bed like some pathetic fool.

And still the wolves edged closer.

"Go away!" Henry shouted, grabbing a clump of dirt and throwing it helplessly at the nearest creature. "What have I ever done to you? Why must you torment me like this?"

The wolves were all around him now, but Henry couldn't help thinking that they were holding back. He waited for the inevitable next strike, yet as the seconds passed he began to wonder whether they were enjoying themselves by toying with him. They wanted him dead, that much was clear, but first they wanted to watch him suffer for as long as possible.

"Do it!" he snarled, shaking with fear as he awaited the next bite, then the next clawing, and finally the end of his miserable and very painful life. "Show me some mercy, though. At least let me die before you start chewing on my bones. Will you give me that? End the misery that I could not end myself!"

He waited, and then – as if in response to some hidden signal – the wolves all turned and raced away at the exact same moment.

"Where are you going?" Henry called after them. "Has the Devil got your tails? Why must you torture me like this?"

***

A few minutes later, as Henry tried to summon the strength to stand, he heard footsteps approaching through the forest. He turned to look, and to his surprise he saw that Clanath was on her way back to him.

"You?" he whispered, as he looked at the strange dirty white gown she was now wearing. "I thought you were gone forever."

"So did I," she replied calmly, stopping in front of him and looking down at his bloodied face. "They've done a lot of damage."

"I thought they were going to finish me off."

"They could have, easily," she said, before tilting her head slightly. "If it had been that simple, however, you would have been dead long before now. It doesn't just matter to them that you die. They also care *how* your end comes."

"What does that mean?" he asked.

"It means that the king of my pack has expressed his grave disappointment in my conduct," she explained. "I spent too much time around you. I let my curiosity take control. I should never have been so weak."

"I'm sorry that I was so fascinating."

"I forgive you," she said with a faint smile, before holding out a hand. "Stand up."

"I'm not sure that I can."

"You can," she said firmly. "We both know

that."

After hesitating for a moment, Henry took her hand and slowly rose. He hated having to reply upon anyone – especially a woman – but finally he managed to stand, even though his legs were shaking and he felt sure that he might fall again at any moment.

"You are in some ways so very typical of your species," she pointed out. "When you are close to life, you think of death, and when you are close to death you think only of life. Why can't you ever make up your mind?"

"And why must you speak in these riddles?" he asked.

"I have learned from you," she told him, tilting her head slightly as tears began to gather in her eyes. "I have allowed myself to be tempted by you, Henry Sobolton. That was wrong of me, and I must prove to the rest of the pack that I have learned my lesson. I must demonstrate my absolute and complete loyalty to my own kind. I have to prove to them that I have not allowed you to change me."

"And how will you do that?"

He waited, but for a moment she merely looked deep into his eyes.

"And how will you do that?" he asked again. "What -"

Suddenly she plunged a knife into his belly.

She quickly twisted the blade and then pulled it out, and blood began to gush from the wound. Letting out a faint gasp, Henry reached out and grabbed her shoulder, trying to hold himself up. When that failed, he dropped down onto his knees as he felt a torrent of hot blood soaking down his body.

"It is done," Clanath said, her voice tense with emotion as she watched Henry's dying moments. "I have shown that I am no traitor to my people."

She paused, before raising the bloodied knife and looking all around.

"Do you see?" she screamed as blood trickled down onto the handle and then onto her fingers. "I have done what you asked! I have shown my allegiance to our pack more clearly and more devoutly than anyone else has ever managed! In this way, I have atoned for my sins and I beg your mercy!"

"There is no answer from them," Henry gasped as blood began to fill his mouth.

"On the contrary," she replied, looking down at him again, "I hear the answer loud and clear. I have done what was required of me." She paused, before stepping back and turning away. "Goodbye, Henry Sobolton," she said as she walked between the trees, still holding the knife. "Do not think that your time here will be forgotten. I will always remember these years as a lesson about the dangers of fraternizing with humans. Believe me, I shall most certainly never make the same mistake again."

Expecting him to shout some last defiant message, she stopped for a moment. Realizing that he'd fallen silent, she turned just in time to see him slumping down against the ground. She furrowed her brow as she heard him talking to himself, and she saw that even though death was close, he was still holding on.

"Do you see them?" he gasped finally. "Please, you have to tell me... are they really here?"

She opened her mouth to ask what he meant, but then she blinked and suddenly she saw a woman and two young girls kneeling next to the dying man. They looked entirely ordinary and unharmed, save for the fact that even from this distance she could tell that they had no scent. The figures were tending to Henry, perhaps comforting him, and after a few seconds Clanath realized that they must be his wife and daughters.

"Yes," she told him, unable to hide the wonder in her voice as tears reached her eyes, "I see them."

"Thank you," he gurgled, looking up at the three women. He tried to say something else, but finally he fell silent and a fraction of a second later he slumped back down.

All three of the women turned to Clanath,

and she understood now that they had finally come to ease their love one's journey to whatever world came next. After watching the scene for a moment, she turned and walked away, dropping the bloodied knife in the process.

"I have done what you asked of me," she said through gritted teeth, as she sensed wolves watching her from all around in the forest. "Now let me rest."

CHAPTER THIRTY

Sobolton, USA – Today...

"OKAY, LET'S CALM DOWN a little," Toby said as he stood in the station's reception area, near the spot where the door had been ripped away. "Everyone settle. The immediate danger's over, the wolf has gone and that guy... I don't know exactly who he was, but he's gone too."

"I still can't get Sheriff Tench on the phone," Carolyn muttered as she set the receiver down. She tried to hide the fact that her hands were shaking. "It's been hours now. I called some of the others out at the investigation sites, but no-one seems to have seen him for a while. If he was on his way back, he should be here by now."

"You can tell a lot about a man by what he

does in a crisis," Toby replied, before turning to look around at the shell-shocked faces of the others. In that moment, he realized that they were waiting for someone to show some leadership. Having always shied away from such lofty ideas before, he now felt – for the very first time in his life – as if he had a duty to take charge. "Now, I don't mean to criticize Sheriff Tench unduly," he continued, warming to his theme, "but the fact is, there's no sign of him and we need to get our shit together."

"I'm sure he'll be here soon," Sheila suggested.

"Well, he's not here *now*," Toby said firmly. "Or is he? Does anyone see him?"

He waited, but he already knew the answer to his question.

"I didn't think so," he added. "We can't afford to sit around and twiddle our thumbs until he decides to show his face. Unless I'm very much mistaken, our station was briefly under siege today and things could have gone a lot worse." He hesitated, wondering how far to push, but he was starting to understand that the others seemed to be lapping up his every word. For the first time, he began to know how it felt to be on the cusp of real power, and he realized that he didn't want this moment to end. "If Sheriff Tench shows up again," he continued, "I'm sure he can explain why he's been completely absent during all of this. In the meantime, however, we need to get on with things. Are you with me?"

A murmur of agreement rippled through the gathered crowd.

"I'm going to keep trying him," Carolyn stammered.

"You do that," Toby said with a faint smile, "and the rest of us are gonna get on with making our town safe. I'm going to pull all the teams away from the cabin and the river. All that dumb stuff can wait. We need boots on the ground right now, and we need people patrolling our streets so that people know they're being kept safe. That big wolf could have attacked more people. Hell, what if it had gone for a child? What if there'd been others? What if they'd attacked the school or the hospital? We came so close to absolute disaster, but I'm not gonna let that happen again. Not on my watch."

"So what exactly do you think we should do?" Sheila asked.

"Good question," he replied. "As it happens, I've already got a plan. I'm going to divide responsibilities up between various groups, and we're going to get out there and show the people of Sobolton that they can rely on us." Looking over at the broken door, he saw a larger crowd starting to gather in the parking lot. "This town is facing a crisis," he continued, "and I've got a horrible feeling that it's not over just yet. That's why we're going to step in and do the job that people expect us to do. And I promise you all one thing... there will be no more wolf attacks in Sobolton. Not now, and not ever. And our first priority is going to be hunting down and killing the wolf that came into our town today."

"Come on, John," Carolyn muttered, trying his number yet again. "Pick up. Where the hell are you?"

***

"Where are you going to go?"

"I don't know," Lisa said, still in the back of the car as Robert drove them along the road leading up and out of Sobolton. "Anywhere. Everywhere. Somewhere safe."

"Where's safe?" he asked, glancing at her reflection in the mirror. "How far do you have to go, to make sure that these things can't reach you?"

"I don't know, but I'm sure it's possible," she told him, looking at the road ahead. "I'll know when we -"

Spotting movement, she saw to her horror that a couple of wolves were stepping out of the forest.

"Watch out!"

Robert slammed his foot on the brake pedal, bringing the vehicle to a juddering halt just as half a dozen more wolves emerged from between the trees and made their way to the middle of the road. Ahead, a full moon was just about visible in the sky.

"What are they doing?" Robert asked.

"Drive through them," Lisa snarled.

"*Through* them?"

"Knock them down," she continued as more wolves appeared. "Go right over them. I don't care what you have to do, but get past them somehow." She waited for Robert to react. "If you won't," she added, "then we'll swap seats and I'll do it myself. With pleasure."

"Mommy, what's happening?" Eloise asked. "What are those wolves doing?"

"They're trying to stop us leaving," Lisa replied, "but they won't succeed."

"There are so many of them," Robert pointed out, as three more wolves stepped out onto the road. A dozen or so were in position now, blocking the way entirely. After a moment he gritted his teeth and took a deep breath. "I'm sorry," he told the car, "I promise I'll get any dents and scratches fixed up just as soon as we're out of this mess. But right now, I'm afraid I need you to be something of a torpedo."

"Do it!" Lisa shouted. "This is our last chance!"

"Here goes nothing," Robert replied, putting the car in gear and then flooring the pedal. "Hold onto your hats!"

The car lurched forward, but only for a fraction of a second before the engine cut out and the power died. Shocked, Robert immediately tried to get the vehicle restarted even as it rolled to a slow stop.

"What's wrong?" Lisa asked.

"This is impossible," he muttered, turning the key again and again, still not managing to get so much as a splutter from the engine. "Greg did the job on her himself, and I trust that man's hands implicitly. He's the best mechanic in the state!"

"It's them," Lisa whispered, watching the wolves that had gathered up ahead. "They know exactly what they're doing. They won't let us leave."

"And how exactly are they stopping us?" Robert asked as he tried the engine again and again.

"We're at the limit of their territory," she told him as fear began to fill her voice. "For some reason, that's often where their power's at its strongest, especially when a lot of them band together."

Robert let go of the key. A moment later the car gently rolled back a few feet and the power returned.

"We'll try a different road," he suggested.

"There's no point," Lisa told him. "They'll have every exit covered. We're too late."

"How can they have *every* exit covered?" he

asked, as he saw a couple of the wolves starting to make their way slowly toward the car. "How many of these damn creatures are there, anyway?"

"You'd be surprised," she replied. "I've always suspected that when they need the numbers, they have a whole army to call on. Michael never took me into the heart of their kingdom, the cabin was always on the periphery. But when push comes to shove, they're going to be able to show some real strength."

"Okay, so what do we do?" Robert asked, tensing as he saw wolves approaching either side of the car. "Lisa, now might be a bad time for me to admit this, but I don't have a limitless supply of silver-tipped canes. In fact, the one we used earlier and left behind was kind of the only one in my possession."

"I'm not sure that'd help us in this situation," she admitted.

Reaching over, Robert carefully locked all the doors.

"And I'm not sure that'll help either," Lisa continued, watching as the wolves – numbering at least thirty now – began to encircle the car, blocking off every possible exit. "There are too many of them, and they're too powerful. Even one of them by itself would be almost impossible to fight against, but with this many..." She turned and looked the other way, and she saw the eyes of all the wolves glaring in at her. Reaching out, she instinctively pulled Eloise closer, at which point she realized that her daughter was trembling. "No-one could fight off this many," she added. "They're too strong."

"So what do we do?" Robert asked as he saw yet more wolves starting to make their way out of the forest. "Lisa? I'm all out of ideas. What do we do to get away from them?"

"I'll think of something."

"What -"

"I said I'll think of something!" she shouted angrily, finally succumbing to panic as she hugged Eloise tight and looked around at the wolves that were now surrounding the car. "I don't know what, but... there has to be a way for us to get out of here!"

Next in this series

**IN HUMAN BONDS
(THE HORRORS OF SOBOLTON BOOK 8)**

Facing the prospect of all-out war between the human and wolf worlds, John and Lisa reluctantly accept that they're going to have to work together. Time's running out, but Lisa's sure that she knows how disaster can be averted. First, though, she needs to face the truth about her terrifying past.

John, meanwhile, is struggling to deal with the changes that even now are coursing through his body. Refusing to accept the truth, he tries to find some way of reversing his condition. There's one person who might be able to help, but Doctor Robert Law seems to be in no fit state to deal with reality.

Dark forces are at work in Sobolton, and an ancient agreement is in danger of collapsing. Glimpsing flashes of a terrifying future, Doctor Law knows better than anyone that the stakes have never been higher. But is an even greater threat lurking in the shadows, waiting to strike?

AMY CROSS

Also by Amy Cross

1689
(The Haunting of Hadlow House book 1)

All Richard Hadlow wants is a happy family and a peaceful home. Having built the perfect house deep in the Kent countryside, now all he needs is a wife. He's about to discover, however, that even the most perfectly-laid plans can go horribly and tragically wrong.

The year is 1689 and England is in the grip of turmoil. A pretender is trying to take the throne, but Richard has no interest in the affairs of his country. He only cares about finding the perfect wife and giving her a perfect life. But someone – or something – at his newly-built house has other ideas. Is Richard's new life about to be destroyed forever?

Hadlow House is brand new, but already there are strange whispers in the corridors and unexplained noises at night. Has Richard been unlucky, is his new wife simply imagining things, or is a dark secret from the past about to rise up and deliver Richard's worst nightmare?
Who wins when the past and the present collide?

AMY CROSS

Also by Amy Cross

The Haunting of Nelson Street
(The Ghosts of Crowford book 1)

Crowford, a sleepy coastal town in the south of England, might seem like an oasis of calm and tranquility. Beneath the surface, however, dark secrets are waiting to claim fresh victims, and ghostly figures plot revenge.

Having finally decided to leave the hustle of London, Daisy and Richard Johnson buy two houses on Nelson Street, a picturesque street in the center of Crowford. One house is perfect and ready to move into, while the other is a fire-ravaged wreck that needs a lot of work. They figure they have plenty of time to work on the damaged house while Daisy recovers from a traumatic event.

Soon, they discover that the two houses share a common link to the past. Something awful once happened on Nelson Street, something that shook the town to its core.

AMY CROSS

Also by Amy Cross

The Revenge of the Mercy Belle
(The Ghosts of Crowford book 2)

The year is 1950, and a great tragedy has struck the town of Crowford. Three local men have been killed in a storm, after their fishing boat the Mercy Belle sank. A mysterious fourth man, however, was rescue. Nobody knows who he is, or what he was doing on the Mercy Belle... and the man has lost his memory.

Five years later, messages from the dead warn of impending doom for Crowford. The ghosts of the Mercy Belle's crew demand revenge, and the whole town is being punished. The fourth man still has no memory of his previous existence, but he's married now and living under the named Edward Smith. As Crowford's suffering continues, the locals begin to turn against him.

What really happened on the night the Mercy Belle sank? Did the fourth man cause the tragedy? And will Crowford survive if this man is not sent to meet his fate?

AMY CROSS

Also by Amy Cross

The Devil, the Witch and the Whore (The Deal book 1)

"Leave the forest alone. Whatever's out there, just let it be. Don't make it angry."

When a horrific discovery is made at the edge of town, Sheriff James Kopperud realizes the answers he seeks might be waiting beyond in the vast forest. But everybody in the town of Deal knows that there's something out there in the forest, something that should never be disturbed. A deal was made long ago, a deal that was supposed to keep the town safe. And if he insists on investigating the murder of a local girl, James is going to have to break that deal and head out into the wilderness.

Meanwhile, James has no idea that his estranged daughter Ramsey has returned to town. Ramsey is running from something, and she thinks she can find safety in the vast tunnel system that runs beneath the forest. Before long, however, Ramsey finds herself coming face to face with creatures that hide in the shadows. One of these creatures is known as the devil, and another is known as the witch. They're both waiting for the whore to arrive, but for very different reasons. And soon Ramsey is offered a terrible deal, one that could save or destroy the entire town, and maybe even the world.

AMY CROSS

Also by Amy Cross

**If You Didn't Like Me Then,
You Probably Won't Like Me Now**

One year ago, Sheryl and her friends did something bad. Really bad. They ritually humiliated local girl Rachel Ritter, before posting the video online for all to see. After that night, Rachel left town and was never seen again. Until now.

Late one night, Sheryl and her friends realize that Rachel's back. At first they think there's on reason to be concerned, but a series of strange events soon convince them that they need to be worried. On the outside, Rachel acts as if all is forgiven, but she's hiding a shocking secret that soon starts to have deadly consequences.

By the time they understand the full horror of Rachel's plans, Sheryl and her friends might be too late to save themselves. Is Rachel really out for revenge? What does she have in store for her tormentors? And just how far is she willing to go? Would she, for example, do something that nobody in all of human history has ever managed to achieve?

If You Didn't Like Me Then, You Probably Won't Like Me Now is a horror novel about the surprising nature of revenge, about the power of hatred, and about the future of humanity.

Also by Amy Cross

The Soul Auction

"I saw a woman on the beach. I watched her face a demon."

Thirty years after her mother's death, Alice Ashcroft is drawn back to the coastal English town of Curridge. Somebody in Curridge has been reviewing Alice's novels online, and in those reviews there have been tantalizing hints at a hidden truth. A truth that seems to be linked to her dead mother.

"Thirty years ago, there was a soul auction."

Once she reaches Curridge, Alice finds strange things happening all around her. Something attacks her car. A figure watches her on the beach at night. And when she tries to find the person who has been reviewing her books, she makes a horrific discovery.

What really happened to Alice's mother thirty years ago? Who was she talking to, just moments before dropping dead on the beach? What caused a huge rockfall that nearly tore a nearby cliff-face in half? And what sinister presence is lurking in the grounds of the local church?

AMY CROSS

CRY OF THE WOLF

Also by Amy Cross

American Coven

He kidnapped three women and held them in his basement. He thought they couldn't fight back. He was wrong...

Snatched from the street near her home, Holly Carter is taken to a rural house and thrown down into a stone basement. She meets two other women who have also been kidnapped, and soon Holly learns about the horrific rituals that take place in the house. Eventually, she's called upstairs to take her place in the ice bath.

As her nightmare continues, however, Holly learns about a mysterious power that exists in the basement, and which the three women might be able to harness. When they finally manage to get through the metal door, however, the women have no idea that their fight for freedom is going to stretch out for more than a decade, or that it will culminate in a final, devastating demonstration of their new-found powers.

Also by Amy Cross

The Ash House

Why would anyone ever return to a haunted house?

For Diane Mercer the answer is simple. She's dying of cancer, and she wants to know once and for all whether ghosts are real.

Heading home with her young son, Diane is determined to find out whether the stories are real. After all, everyone else claimed to see and hear strange things in the house over the years. Everyone except Diane had some kind of experience in the house, or in the little ash house in the yard.

As Diane explores the house where she grew up, however, her son is exploring the yard and the forest. And while his mother might be struggling to come to terms with her own impending death, Daniel Mercer is puzzled by fleeting appearances of a strange little girl who seems drawn to the ash house, and by strange, rasping coughs that he keeps hearing at night.

The Ash House is a horror novel about a woman who desperately wants to know what will happen to her when she dies, and about a boy who uncovers the shocking truth about a young girl's murder.

Also by Amy Cross

Haunted

Twenty years ago, the ghost of a dead little girl drove Sheriff Michael Blaine to his death.

Now, that same ghost is coming for his daughter.

Returning to the small town where she grew up, Alex Roberts is determined to live a normal, quiet life. For the residents of Railham, however, she's an unwelcome reminder of the town's darkest hour.

Twenty years ago, nine-year-old Mo Garvey was found brutally murdered in a nearby forest. Everyone thinks that Alex's father was responsible, but if the killer was brought to justice, why is the ghost of Mo Garvey still after revenge?

And how far will the real killer go to protect his secret, when Alex starts getting closer to the truth?

Haunted is a horror novel about a woman who has to face her past, about a town that would rather forget, and about a little girl who refuses to let death stand in her way.

AMY CROSS

Also by Amy Cross

The Curse of Wetherley House

"If you walk through that door, Evil Mary will get you."

When she agrees to visit a supposedly haunted house with an old friend, Rosie assumes she'll encounter nothing more scary than a few creaks and bumps in the night. Even the legend of Evil Mary doesn't put her off. After all, she knows ghosts aren't real. But when Mary makes her first appearance, Rosie realizes she might already be trapped.

For more than a century, Wetherley House has been cursed. A horrific encounter on a remote road in the late 1800's has already caused a chain of misery and pain for all those who live at the house. Wetherley House was abandoned long ago, after a terrible discovery in the basement, something has remained undetected within its room. And even the local children know that Evil Mary waits in the house for anyone foolish enough to walk through the front door.

Before long, Rosie realizes that her entire life has been defined by the spirit of a woman who died in agony. Can she become the first person to escape Evil Mary, or will she fall victim to the same fate as the house's other occupants?

AMY CROSS

BOOKS BY AMY CROSS

1. Dark Season: The Complete First Series (2011)
2. Werewolves of Soho (Lupine Howl book 1) (2012)
3. Werewolves of the Other London (Lupine Howl book 2) (2012)
4. Ghosts: The Complete Series (2012)
5. Dark Season: The Complete Second Series (2012)
6. The Children of Black Annis (Lupine Howl book 3) (2012)
7. Destiny of the Last Wolf (Lupine Howl book 4) (2012)
8. Asylum (The Asylum Trilogy book 1) (2012)
9. Dark Season: The Complete Third Series (2013)
10. Devil's Briar (2013)
11. Broken Blue (The Broken Trilogy book 1) (2013)
12. The Night Girl (2013)
13. Days 1 to 4 (Mass Extinction Event book 1) (2013)
14. Days 5 to 8 (Mass Extinction Event book 2) (2013)
15. The Library (The Library Chronicles book 1) (2013)
16. American Coven (2013)
17. Werewolves of Sangreth (Lupine Howl book 5) (2013)
18. Broken White (The Broken Trilogy book 2) (2013)
19. Grave Girl (Grave Girl book 1) (2013)
20. Other People's Bodies (2013)
21. The Shades (2013)
22. The Vampire's Grave and Other Stories (2013)
23. Darper Danver: The Complete First Series (2013)
24. The Hollow Church (2013)
25. The Dead and the Dying (2013)
26. Days 9 to 16 (Mass Extinction Event book 3) (2013)
27. The Girl Who Never Came Back (2013)
28. Ward Z (The Ward Z Series book 1) (2013)
29. Journey to the Library (The Library Chronicles book 2) (2014)
30. The Vampires of Tor Cliff Asylum (2014)
31. The Family Man (2014)
32. The Devil's Blade (2014)
33. The Immortal Wolf (Lupine Howl book 6) (2014)
34. The Dying Streets (Detective Laura Foster book 1) (2014)
35. The Stars My Home (2014)
36. The Ghost in the Rain and Other Stories (2014)
37. Ghosts of the River Thames (The Robinson Chronicles book 1) (2014)
38. The Wolves of Cur'eath (2014)
39. Days 46 to 53 (Mass Extinction Event book 4) (2014)
40. The Man Who Saw the Face of the World (2014)
41. The Art of Dying (Detective Laura Foster book 2) (2014)
42. Raven Revivals (Grave Girl book 2) (2014)

AMY CROSS

43. Arrival on Thaxos (Dead Souls book 1) (2014)
44. Birthright (Dead Souls book 2) (2014)
45. A Man of Ghosts (Dead Souls book 3) (2014)
46. The Haunting of Hardstone Jail (2014)
47. A Very Respectable Woman (2015)
48. Better the Devil (2015)
49. The Haunting of Marshall Heights (2015)
50. Terror at Camp Everbee (The Ward Z Series book 2) (2015)
51. Guided by Evil (Dead Souls book 4) (2015)
52. Child of a Bloodied Hand (Dead Souls book 5) (2015)
53. Promises of the Dead (Dead Souls book 6) (2015)
54. Days 54 to 61 (Mass Extinction Event book 5) (2015)
55. Angels in the Machine (The Robinson Chronicles book 2) (2015)
56. The Curse of Ah-Qal's Tomb (2015)
57. Broken Red (The Broken Trilogy book 3) (2015)
58. The Farm (2015)
59. Fallen Heroes (Detective Laura Foster book 3) (2015)
60. The Haunting of Emily Stone (2015)
61. Cursed Across Time (Dead Souls book 7) (2015)
62. Destiny of the Dead (Dead Souls book 8) (2015)
63. The Death of Jennifer Kazakos (Dead Souls book 9) (2015)
64. Alice Isn't Well (Death Herself book 1) (2015)
65. Annie's Room (2015)
66. The House on Everley Street (Death Herself book 2) (2015)
67. Meds (The Asylum Trilogy book 2) (2015)
68. Take Me to Church (2015)
69. Ascension (Demon's Grail book 1) (2015)
70. The Priest Hole (Nykolas Freeman book 1) (2015)
71. Eli's Town (2015)
72. The Horror of Raven's Briar Orphanage (Dead Souls book 10) (2015)
73. The Witch of Thaxos (Dead Souls book 11) (2015)
74. The Rise of Ashalla (Dead Souls book 12) (2015)
75. Evolution (Demon's Grail book 2) (2015)
76. The Island (The Island book 1) (2015)
77. The Lighthouse (2015)
78. The Cabin (The Cabin Trilogy book 1) (2015)
79. At the Edge of the Forest (2015)
80. The Devil's Hand (2015)
81. The 13th Demon (Demon's Grail book 3) (2016)
82. After the Cabin (The Cabin Trilogy book 2) (2016)
83. The Border: The Complete Series (2016)
84. The Dead Ones (Death Herself book 3) (2016)
85. A House in London (2016)
86. Persona (The Island book 2) (2016)

87. Battlefield (Nykolas Freeman book 2) (2016)
88. Perfect Little Monsters and Other Stories (2016)
89. The Ghost of Shapley Hall (2016)
90. The Blood House (2016)
91. The Death of Addie Gray (2016)
92. The Girl With Crooked Fangs (2016)
93. Last Wrong Turn (2016)
94. The Body at Auercliff (2016)
95. The Printer From Hell (2016)
96. The Dog (2016)
97. The Nurse (2016)
98. The Haunting of Blackwych Grange (2016)
99. Twisted Little Things and Other Stories (2016)
100. The Horror of Devil's Root Lake (2016)
101. The Disappearance of Katie Wren (2016)
102. B&B (2016)
103. The Bride of Ashbyrn House (2016)
104. The Devil, the Witch and the Whore (The Deal Trilogy book 1) (2016)
105. The Ghosts of Lakeforth Hotel (2016)
106. The Ghost of Longthorn Manor and Other Stories (2016)
107. Laura (2017)
108. The Murder at Skellin Cottage (Jo Mason book 1) (2017)
109. The Curse of Wetherley House (2017)
110. The Ghosts of Hexley Airport (2017)
111. The Return of Rachel Stone (Jo Mason book 2) (2017)
112. Haunted (2017)
113. The Vampire of Downing Street and Other Stories (2017)
114. The Ash House (2017)
115. The Ghost of Molly Holt (2017)
116. The Camera Man (2017)
117. The Soul Auction (2017)
118. The Abyss (The Island book 3) (2017)
119. Broken Window (The House of Jack the Ripper book 1) (2017)
120. In Darkness Dwell (The House of Jack the Ripper book 2) (2017)
121. Cradle to Grave (The House of Jack the Ripper book 3) (2017)
122. The Lady Screams (The House of Jack the Ripper book 4) (2017)
123. A Beast Well Tamed (The House of Jack the Ripper book 5) (2017)
124. Doctor Charles Grazier (The House of Jack the Ripper book 6) (2017)
125. The Raven Watcher (The House of Jack the Ripper book 7) (2017)
126. The Final Act (The House of Jack the Ripper book 8) (2017)
127. Stephen (2017)
128. The Spider (2017)
129. The Mermaid's Revenge (2017)
130. The Girl Who Threw Rocks at the Devil (2018)

AMY CROSS

131. Friend From the Internet (2018)
132. Beautiful Familiar (2018)
133. One Night at a Soul Auction (2018)
134. 16 Frames of the Devil's Face (2018)
135. The Haunting of Caldgrave House (2018)
136. Like Stones on a Crow's Back (The Deal Trilogy book 2) (2018)
137. Room 9 and Other Stories (2018)
138. The Gravest Girl of All (Grave Girl book 3) (2018)
139. Return to Thaxos (Dead Souls book 13) (2018)
140. The Madness of Annie Radford (The Asylum Trilogy book 3) (2018)
141. The Haunting of Briarwych Church (Briarwych book 1) (2018)
142. I Just Want You To Be Happy (2018)
143. Day 100 (Mass Extinction Event book 6) (2018)
144. The Horror of Briarwych Church (Briarwych book 2) (2018)
145. The Ghost of Briarwych Church (Briarwych book 3) (2018)
146. Lights Out (2019)
147. Apocalypse (The Ward Z Series book 3) (2019)
148. Days 101 to 108 (Mass Extinction Event book 7) (2019)
149. The Haunting of Daniel Bayliss (2019)
150. The Purchase (2019)
151. Harper's Hotel Ghost Girl (Death Herself book 4) (2019)
152. The Haunting of Aldburn House (2019)
153. Days 109 to 116 (Mass Extinction Event book 8) (2019)
154. Bad News (2019)
155. The Wedding of Rachel Blaine (2019)
156. Dark Little Wonders and Other Stories (2019)
157. The Music Man (2019)
158. The Vampire Falls (Three Nights of the Vampire book 1) (2019)
159. The Other Ann (2019)
160. The Butcher's Husband and Other Stories (2019)
161. The Haunting of Lannister Hall (2019)
162. The Vampire Burns (Three Nights of the Vampire book 2) (2019)
163. Days 195 to 202 (Mass Extinction Event book 9) (2019)
164. Escape From Hotel Necro (2019)
165. The Vampire Rises (Three Nights of the Vampire book 3) (2019)
166. Ten Chimes to Midnight: A Collection of Ghost Stories (2019)
167. The Strangler's Daughter (2019)
168. The Beast on the Tracks (2019)
169. The Haunting of the King's Head (2019)
170. I Married a Serial Killer (2019)
171. Your Inhuman Heart (2020)
172. Days 203 to 210 (Mass Extinction Event book 10) (2020)
173. The Ghosts of David Brook (2020)
174. Days 349 to 356 (Mass Extinction Event book 11) (2020)

175. The Horror at Criven Farm (2020)
176. Mary (2020)
177. The Middlewych Experiment (Chaos Gear Annie book 1) (2020)
178. Days 357 to 364 (Mass Extinction Event book 12) (2020)
179. Day 365: The Final Day (Mass Extinction Event book 13) (2020)
180. The Haunting of Hathaway House (2020)
181. Don't Let the Devil Know Your Name (2020)
182. The Legend of Rinth (2020)
183. The Ghost of Old Coal House (2020)
184. The Root (2020)
185. I'm Not a Zombie (2020)
186. The Ghost of Annie Close (2020)
187. The Disappearance of Lonnie James (2020)
188. The Curse of the Langfords (2020)
189. The Haunting of Nelson Street (The Ghosts of Crowford 1) (2020)
190. Strange Little Horrors and Other Stories (2020)
191. The House Where She Died (2020)
192. The Revenge of the Mercy Belle (The Ghosts of Crowford 2) (2020)
193. The Ghost of Crowford School (The Ghosts of Crowford book 3) (2020)
194. The Haunting of Hardlocke House (2020)
195. The Cemetery Ghost (2020)
196. You Should Have Seen Her (2020)
197. The Portrait of Sister Elsa (The Ghosts of Crowford book 4) (2021)
198. The House on Fisher Street (2021)
199. The Haunting of the Crowford Hoy (The Ghosts of Crowford 5) (2021)
200. Trill (2021)
201. The Horror of the Crowford Empire (The Ghosts of Crowford 6) (2021)
202. Out There (The Ted Armitage Trilogy book 1) (2021)
203. The Nightmare of Crowford Hospital (The Ghosts of Crowford 7) (2021)
204. Twist Valley (The Ted Armitage Trilogy book 2) (2021)
205. The Great Beyond (The Ted Armitage Trilogy book 3) (2021)
206. The Haunting of Edward House (2021)
207. The Curse of the Crowford Grand (The Ghosts of Crowford 8) (2021)
208. How to Make a Ghost (2021)
209. The Ghosts of Crossley Manor (The Ghosts of Crowford 9) (2021)
210. The Haunting of Matthew Thorne (2021)
211. The Siege of Crowford Castle (The Ghosts of Crowford 10) (2021)
212. Daisy: The Complete Series (2021)
213. Bait (Bait book 1) (2021)
214. Origin (Bait book 2) (2021)
215. Heretic (Bait book 3) (2021)
216. Anna's Sister (2021)
217. The Haunting of Quist House (The Rose Files 1) (2021)
218. The Haunting of Crowford Station (The Ghosts of Crowford 11) (2022)

AMY CROSS

219. The Curse of Rosie Stone (2022)
220. The First Order (The Chronicles of Sister June book 1) (2022)
221. The Second Veil (The Chronicles of Sister June book 2) (2022)
222. The Graves of Crowford Rise (The Ghosts of Crowford 12) (2022)
223. Dead Man: The Resurrection of Morton Kane (2022)
224. The Third Beast (The Chronicles of Sister June book 3) (2022)
225. The Legend of the Crossley Stag (The Ghosts of Crowford 13) (2022)
226. One Star (2022)
227. The Ghost in Room 119 (2022)
228. The Fourth Shadow (The Chronicles of Sister June book 4) (2022)
229. The Soldier Without a Past (Dead Souls book 14) (2022)
230. The Ghosts of Marsh House (2022)
231. Wax: The Complete Series (2022)
232. The Phantom of Crowford Theatre (The Ghosts of Crowford 14) (2022)
233. The Haunting of Hurst House (Mercy Willow book 1) (2022)
234. Blood Rains Down From the Sky (The Deal Trilogy book 3) (2022)
235. The Spirit on Sidle Street (Mercy Willow book 2) (2022)
236. The Ghost of Gower Grange (Mercy Willow book 3) (2022)
237. The Curse of Clute Cottage (Mercy Willow book 4) (2022)
238. The Haunting of Anna Jenkins (Mercy Willow book 5) (2023)
239. The Death of Mercy Willow (Mercy Willow book 6) (2023)
240. Angel (2023)
241. The Eyes of Maddy Park (2023)
242. If You Didn't Like Me Then, You Probably Won't Like Me Now (2023)
243. The Terror of Torfork Tower (Mercy Willow 7) (2023)
244. The Phantom of Payne Priory (Mercy Willow 8) (2023)
245. The Devil on Davis Drive (Mercy Willow 9) (2023)
246. The Haunting of the Ghost of Tom Bell (Mercy Willow 10) (2023)
247. The Other Ghost of Gower Grange (Mercy Willow 11) (2023)
248. The Haunting of Olive Atkins (Mercy Willow 12) (2023)
249. The End of Marcy Willow (Mercy Willow 13) (2023)
250. The Last Haunted House on Mars and Other Stories (2023)
251. 1689 (The Haunting of Hadlow House 1) (2023)
252. 1722 (The Haunting of Hadlow House 2) (2023)
253. 1775 (The Haunting of Hadlow House 3) (2023)
254. The Terror of Crowford Carnival (The Ghosts of Crowford 15) (2023)
255. 1800 (The Haunting of Hadlow House 4) (2023)
256. 1837 (The Haunting of Hadlow House 5) (2023)
257. 1885 (The Haunting of Hadlow House 6) (2023)
258. 1901 (The Haunting of Hadlow House 7) (2023)
259. 1918 (The Haunting of Hadlow House 8) (2023)
260. The Secret of Adam Grey (The Ghosts of Crowford 16) (2023)
261. 1926 (The Haunting of Hadlow House 9) (2023)
262. 1939 (The Haunting of Hadlow House 10) (2023)

263. The Fifth Tomb (The Chronicles of Sister June 5) (2023)
264. 1966 (The Haunting of Hadlow House 11) (2023)
265. 1999 (The Haunting of Hadlow House 12) (2023)
266. The Hauntings of Mia Rush (2023)
267. 2024 (The Haunting of Hadlow House 13) (2024)
268. The Sixth Window (The Chronicles of Sister June 6) (2024)
269. Little Miss Dead (The Horrors of Sobolton 1) (2024)
270. Swan Territory (The Horrors of Sobolton 2) (2024)
271. Dead Widow Road (The Horrors of Sobolton 3) (2024)
272. The Haunting of Stryke Brothers (The Ghosts of Crowford 17) (2024)
273. In a Lonely Grave (The Horrors of Sobolton 4) (2024)
274. Electrification (The Horrors of Sobolton 5) (2024)
275. Man on the Moon (The Horrors of Sobolton 6) (2024)
276. The Haunting of Styre House (The Smythe Trilogy book 1) (2024)
277. The Curse of Bloodacre Farm (The Smythe Trilogy book 2) (2024)
278. The Horror of Styre House (The Smythe Trilogy book 3) (2024)
279. Cry of the Wolf (The Horrors of Sobolton 7) (2024)
280. A Cuckoo in Winter (2024)

AMY CROSS

For more information, visit:

www.amycross.com

AMY CROSS

Printed in Great Britain
by Amazon